**A novelization by J.J. Gardner
Based on the screen story and
screenplay by Ed Solomon**

SCHOLASTIC INC.

New York   Toronto   London   Auckland   Sydney

Visit the Sony website at www.sony.com

ISBN 0-590-34418-8

12 11 10 9 8 7 6 5 4 3 2 1   7 8 9/9 0 1 2/0

Cover and color insert designed by Joan Ferrigno

Printed in the U.S.A.   40

First Scholastic printing, July 1997

Prologue: The Border

The driver of the van glanced up at the star-filled night sky and then back down at the road. What he saw momentarily startled him. Either there was a cluster of stars on the road up ahead or he was crazy. Could be an optical illusion, he thought. He blinked a couple of times, but the stars were still there.

Something was wrong. Very wrong. These late-night over-the-border runs had given him a sixth sense. The kind that comes with the knowledge that your vehicle could be spot-checked by the Feds at any second. The Feds who worked this route were good at their jobs, and the driver knew that. They crept up on you. They were like insects, these Feds, the kind that splatter across your windshield suddenly and without warning as you're racing across the state line.

Then he realized: Those aren't stars up ahead. They're headlights. They're Feds.

The driver could sense the tense emotions of his

cargo, a dozen Mexican men who sat huddled in the back of the van. They were trying their best to remain silent, but in that silence the driver could feel their fear. They were good men but also desperate. They had paid their life's savings for a ride across the border into the United States. A chance to get a job and a good wage. To perhaps bring their families across later.

But as the driver slowed the van, he could feel their fear grow.

"Let me do the talking," he told them in Spanish. But even as he brought the van to a stop, he knew it was hopeless. None of these men had a legal right to be crossing the border into Texas. And he was breaking the law by helping them.

"Well, if it isn't good old Nick," said the leader of the group of INS officers as he approached the van. Behind him, eight other men in dark suits waited by their cars. The driver didn't know the others, but he knew the one who had approached him. It was Janus. "What a surprise," the agent continued. "Where you comin' from?"

"I was fishing in Cuernavaca," said Nick snidely. Both men knew it was a lie.

"Sure you were," replied Janus. "What do you say we have a look at your catch?"

By then the other agents had gone to the back of the van and opened the door. One by one the Mexican men filed out, their heads hung low.

Agent Janus shook his head. "What do you get,

Nick?" he asked the driver. "Hundred bucks a head? Two hundred? I hope you saved it all for your lawyer, 'cause you're gonna need it."

Nick knew what was coming next. He could already anticipate the cold steel of the handcuffs that Janus would soon lock around his wrists. But it was just as Nick felt his wrists tense that he heard an approaching motor.

A boxy black 1986 LTD had suddenly come barreling down the road. The car pulled hard to the right and squealed sideways, spraying dirt and dust as it screeched to a full halt. Two men got out. Both were dressed in plain black suits, crisp white shirts, simple black ties, and shiny black shoes.

"We'll take it from here," said one of the Men in Black.

"Who are you?" asked Agent Janus.

The Men in Black flashed their identification cards. "Immigration and Naturalization Service, Division Six," one of them said.

Agent Janus looked confused. "Division Six? I never heard of Division Six."

"Really?" asked the first man in black. Ignoring Agent Janus, the man walked down the row of immigrants, smiling at each one as he went. "What're we thinking, Dee?" the man asked his partner.

"Tough call, Kay," replied Dee.

Kay spoke to each immigrant in Spanish as he moved up and down the line.

3

"Hey, what's up? How are you?" he asked one frightened-looking immigrant in a friendly voice.

"Don't worry, grandma," he said to an old woman. *"Welcome to the United States."*

When he came to the fifth man, his smile disappeared and his face hardened.

"What do you say if I break your face?" he said.

The man smiled and nodded.

Kay grabbed the immigrant hard by the shoulder, satisfied he had found the one he was looking for. "You don't understand a word of Spanish, do you?"

The immigrant nodded and smiled again.

"We got a winner," Kay told Dee. Then he told the other immigrants that they were free to go.

"Sir, you just can't —" Agent Janus started to say in protest.

"Don't 'sir' me," replied Kay, holding tight to the immigrant he had chosen. "You have no *idea* who you're dealing with! We're gonna have a little chat with our friend here. You boys can hit the road . . . and keep protecting us from dangerous aliens."

With that, the two Men in Black led their captive away from the road and over a small rise. Now they were hidden from view. Dee pulled out an enormous handgun and aimed it at the immigrant.

"I think you jumped off the bus in the wrong part of town, *amigo*," Kay told the immigrant. "In fact, I'll bet dollars to *pesos* that you're not from anywhere *near* here."

Kay aimed a small mechanical device at the immigrant and pressed a button. A high-powered laser beam shot out from the device and vaporized the immigrant's clothes. As the clothes disintegrated, so did some of the immigrant's skin. It was as if the man's skin and clothes were made of the same kind of material. When the material was completely gone, Kay and Dee knew their hunch was right.

The immigrant wasn't a man at all. It was a creature. A short, inhuman-looking thing about four feet tall with a snout and rows of scaly, snail-like tentacles. It held its human head on a pole. From out of its neck, two thin stalks with moving eyes looked helplessly at its captors.

Kay recognized the creature right away. "*Mikey!*" he said, feeling like the cat who had just eaten the canary. "When did they let *you* out of jail?"

Mikey replied, not in English or Spanish, but with a series of grunts, squeaks, and saliva. His native language.

Kay rolled his eyes. He had heard it all before. "Political refugee?" he translated. Then he skeptically added: "Right."

"You know how many treaty articles you just violated?" Dee asked the creature.

Mikey let out one lame squeak.

"One?" laughed Kay. "Try *seven*."

"From unauthorized immigration to failure to properly inoculate prior to landing," explained Dee.

"Okay," Kay said to the alien. "Hand me your head and put up your arms."

Mikey was now holding his human head in his hands. He was just about to pass it to them, when a terrified gasp came from behind. Kay and Dee swirled around. It was Agent Janus. He had seen everything.

In the confusion, Mikey seized the opportunity to flee. He knocked Dee's gun out of his hand, let out a horrible screech, and headed straight for Janus.

"Dee! Shoot him!" ordered Kay.

Dee struggled to pick up the gun, his hands shaking.

"Come on, Dee," Kay said. "Do it!"

Nothing. Kay moved quickly. He aimed his gun at the fleeing monstrosity and fired. The beam from his gun hit his target straight on. Mikey exploded into a sizzling geyser of blue goo that splattered everywhere, including on Agent Janus's face.

Janus was in shock. He was shaking. His skin had gone white. His eyes wouldn't even blink.

"Th-that wasn't — wasn't —" he muttered as Kay approached.

"Human, I know," said Kay, finishing the sentence. He took out his handkerchief and began wiping alien goo off Agent Janus's clothes.

Just then several other federal agents came running over the rise to investigate the strange goings-on.

"Okay, everybody," shouted Kay. "Situation's under control. Calm down. If you'll just give me your attention for a moment, I'll tell you what happened." He pulled out a small metal tube about the size of a pocket cassette recorder.

"This is called a neuralyzer," he explained to the shell-shocked Janus. He set the device to level 8. "A gift from some friends from out of town. The red eye here isolates and measures the electronic impulses in your brain. More specifically, the ones for memory."

Within minutes the group of federal agents was surrounded by six more men dressed in black just like Kay and Dee. All the men wore sunglasses.

"Gimme a splay burn on the perimeter, please," Kay told the new Men in Black. "Holes at forty, sixty, and eighty."

One of the Men in Black aimed a flamethrower.

"What's going on here?!" demanded one of the federal agents.

"Exactly the right question," replied Kay. "And the answer lies right here. Pay attention."

Kay held up the neuralyzer. Then he reached into his pocket and put on his own pair of black sunglasses. Dee did the same.

"Who are you, really?" Agent Janus asked Kay.

"Really? I'm just a figment of your imagination."

Kay pressed a button on the neuralyzer. A blinding flash, not more than a second long, seared the eyeballs of the federal agents.

"We're such a gullible breed," quipped Kay. He knew the neuralyzer was taking effect, erasing the agents' minds of everything they had just witnessed.

Meanwhile, the Men in Black sent a blast from the flamethrower, scorching the area. All visible remains of Mikey were now gone. All that was left was a black, burned landscape.

Seconds later, the federal agents began to come around. Their eyesight returned, though their heads were groggy.

"I mean it, fellas," Kay told them. "You're lucky to be alive after a blast like that."

The agents looked around in confusion.

"What blast?" asked Janus.

Kay looked at Dee and smiled. The Feds could not remember anything that had happened.

"Underground gas main, genius," Kay explained to the dizzy agent. "You guys need to exercise more caution before discharging your firearms. Especially you."

The agents accepted Kay's story without dispute. They returned to their cars.

Kay looked down at his neuralyzer and smiled. *Works every time*, he thought, pleased.

Suddenly, Kay realized that Dee had moved away and was sitting by himself on a rock, staring up at the night sky. His partner looked tired. And old. As if the years and the job had caught up with him.

"I'm sorry," said Dee as Kay approached him. "About . . . back there."

"Happens," Kay said with a shrug.

"Didn't used to. The spirit's willing, but the rest of me . . ." Dee held up his hand. It was trembling with age. He looked up at the night sky. "They're beautiful, aren't they?"

"What?" asked Kay, looking up as well.

"The stars," replied Dee. "We never just — *look* anymore. You know what, Kay? I'm going to miss the chase."

So he's decided, thought Kay. *This was it. Dee's last mission.*

"You won't miss it," Kay said quietly. "You won't even remember it." He aimed his neuralyzer at Dee.

1.
The Chase

James Edwards couldn't understand it. No matter how fast he ran, the perpetrator ran faster. No matter how high he jumped, the perp jumped higher. *If I don't catch this perp*, thought Edwards, as he chased the criminal through the rush hour crowd in Grand Central Station, *I'm turnin' in my badge.*

His partner had already given up back on Forty-ninth Street. That was to be expected. His partner was older, not to mention fatter. "All yours, Edwards," his partner had called, breathlessly collapsing against a building.

Edwards made it a habit never to depend on partners. From the moment they saw the perp, Edwards knew he would end up doing the chase alone. The perp was a maniac, a psycho. He was running up and down Madison Avenue, yelling something about the world coming to an end. Edwards had heard it all too many times before. The guy was out of his mind.

11

I'm only human, Edwards told himself as he chased the nutcase out of Grand Central Station to the transverse bridge that rose above Park Avenue. Still, he couldn't shake the notion that there was something different about this perp. The guy was fast. Really fast.

"Stop! NYPD!" Edwards shouted, identifying himself again. That was procedure. Wasted breath. The perp didn't slow down. Instead he leaped over the side of the bridge, a straight thirty-foot drop. The perp landed, barely stumbling, and continued to flee down Forty-first Street.

Edwards, too, hurdled the guardrail. His fall was broken by a passing double-decker bus filled with tourists. *No time to flash the badge,* he thought. He raced down the winding stairs of the moving bus and jumped off, nearly twisting his ankle as he landed on the sidewalk.

The perp was ahead of him now.

"This guy's making me sweat up my gear," he muttered in frustration, his thoughts almost drowned out by the blaring New York City traffic noise. A newspaper truck rumbled by and Edwards decided he needed its help. He ran and leaped onto its back door, staying with the truck for several blocks until it reached the perp, now headed uptown on Madison Avenue.

"Yo, man," Edwards shouted to the perp. "Your luck just ran out." And with that he leaped off the back of the truck and made the tackle. Both men went somersaulting across the sidewalk. Edwards ended up on top, his handcuffs ready.

"He's coming! He's coming!" the perp shouted. He seemed genuinely terrified.

"And when he gets here, I'll kick his butt, too," said Edwards as he started to cuff the perp.

The perp squirmed, his eyes blinking wildly with fear. Edwards had never seen eyes quite like these before. Then he realized that it wasn't the eyes that were strange. It was the eyelids. The perp had two sets of them, like a cat. One set was normal. But underneath was another set of milky-white, translucent ones.

Edwards paused, momentarily distracted by the eyes. That was all the time the perp needed to pull out a gun. Like his eyes, the perp's gun was also unusual. It was long and flat, covered with lots of switches and gizmos, and its trigger seemed to be on the top instead of the bottom.

Reacting quickly, Edwards batted the gun out of the perp's hands. It went flying against a stone wall.

Then it disintegrated into a million tiny bits.

Again Edwards became distracted. Again the perp seized the moment. He punched Edwards in the gut and made a run for it. Edwards grabbed his side in pain but staggered after the perp.

Edwards had been caught off guard and he knew it. It was unprofessional. He was a cop, not a citizen. So what if the perp had feline eyelids? So what if he was almost shot by a gun that looked like it came from outer space? His job was to capture and arrest nutcases like this, not let them get away.

Thoughts like these raced through his mind as he chased the perp to the Guggenheim Museum. But instead of running into the museum, the perp began to scale the outside wall. It was the most amazing thing Edwards had ever seen. The perp moved so quickly and lightly, Edwards would have sworn he was an insect . . . if he hadn't known better!

Edwards entered the museum and ran past startled spectators who were strolling casually past strange and colorful works of modern art. Up he went, winding around the swirling rotunda that climbed toward the top floor of the museum.

Edwards finally reached the perp on the roof of the museum. The perp was cornered. Edwards felt good. He wouldn't let anything distract him now. He pulled out his gun and aimed it.

"Wass up?" he asked the perp, trying to catch his breath.

"He's coming!" the perp shouted at Edwards. "He's coming because I failed! And now he'll kill *me*, too!"

"Stop!" ordered Edwards. The perp was inching his way toward the edge of the roof.

"You don't understand," pleaded the perp. "*The world is gonna end!*"

Edwards moved toward the perp. But it was too late. The perp fell over the edge. Edwards lunged forward and caught him by the hands. He looked into the perp's eyes as they rolled back into his head. Then the other eyelids, the filmy second set, suddenly closed. The perp tore his hands out from under Edwards's hands and jumped over the side of the building. Edwards could only hear him scream to his death.

2.
The Man in Black

"**P**erpetrator then blinked two sets of eyelids," repeated the chief police inspector. "You mean blinked with both eyes?"

"No, sir," replied Edwards. "He blinked once with one set, then again with another completely different set."

"Sort of low beam, high beam," said Edwards's partner, sounding just as skeptical as the chief.

They were sitting in the chief's office, Edwards and his partner. The perp's body had been taken to the morgue, and now Edwards had to explain how he died. There were some elements of the story Edwards didn't even believe himself.

"Was that before or after he drew a weapon which you claim evaporated into a million pieces?" asked the chief.

"After, sir," replied Edwards. He could tell the chief was having a hard time swallowing the report.

"And why do you suppose none of the other officers saw either of these two events?" asked the chief.

"'Cause some of the other officers are a little soggy in the midsection," Edwards said, glancing at his heavyset partner. "They couldn't keep up, sir."

"Hey, Edwards," started his partner. "If you were half the man I am —"

"What do you mean?" replied Edwards. "I *am* half the man you are."

At that, Edward's partner became angry. He would have started a fight if the chief hadn't dragged him out of the office to cool down. When they were gone, Edwards thought of the day's events with dismay. He momentarily put himself in the chief's place and realized that his story didn't wash. *What had happened, then?* he wondered. *Was it all some crazy optical illusion?*

"I believe you," interrupted a voice from behind. Edwards spun around. It was Laurel Weaver, the deputy medical examiner. He had met the pretty young doctor several times while investigating other cases. "I just finished opening him up," Dr. Weaver continued. "Find me in the morgue and I'll tell you what I found."

She turned around and started out of the office.

"Hey, wait a minute —" called Edwards. He twisted in his chair to get a better look at the medical examiner, but she had already disappeared. Suddenly, the hallway outside of the interrogation

17

room was filled with a bright flash of light. It was blinding.

When Edwards's eyes cleared, a man he had never seen before was standing at the door. The man was dressed completely in black.

"Some night, huh?" said the man, closing the door behind him.

"Oh, yeah," replied Edwards. "Some night." He assumed the man was a new detective assigned to ask him some more questions about the perp.

"They were gills," said the man. "Not eyelids."

Edwards threw the man a quizzical look. "Who are you?" he asked.

"Just call me Kay. Did he say anything to you?"

"Yeah, sure, Kay," Edwards replied, scoffing. "He said the world was coming to an end."

"Did he say when?"

Edwards looked at Kay. Was the guy being serious?

"Would you recognize the weapon if you saw it again?" the man asked Edwards.

"Absolutely," replied Edwards.

"Let's take a ride."

"Wait a minute," said Edwards. "I've got a ton of paperwork."

"It's all taken care of," said Kay. At that point the chief stuck his head in and gave Edwards a thumbs-up.

"Good work, Edwards," said the chief.

Edwards knew something was going on. Whoever this guy in black was, he had a lot of pull.

"So you ran that guy down on foot?" Kay asked Edwards as he led him out of the office. "That's tough. That's double tough."

Edwards followed him into a plain black LTD in the precinct parking lot.

"So, who you with?" asked Edwards as the car pulled out of the lot. "You got the plain clothes, the government-issued wheels. Secret Service? CIA?"

"Nothing is what it seems, kid," Kay replied tersely. "I'm with a secret organization that monitors and polices alien activity on Earth."

"Yeah, right," Edwards said skeptically.

Kay stopped the car. Edwards looked around. They were in front of Jeebs's place, the pawnshop. Edwards knew it well. A local dump spot for petty thieves. The kind that stole Rolex watches off businessmen as they waited for their trains during rush hour. Edwards was confused. Jeebs was strictly small time. What would he have to do with illegal aliens or fancy guns?

"*This* is where we're going?" asked Edwards as he followed Kay toward the shop. "Jack Jeebs? Guy buys chains from snatchers. Doesn't even *sell* guns."

"Really?"

"All right," said Edwards in a demanding tone

of voice. "If you think it's worth shaking him up, fine. I'll do my thing. Then I want some answers."

"Do your *thing*, kid," said Kay as they entered the shop.

Edwards had been inside Jeebs's shop many times before. It was one of those small storefronts overcrowded with used trinkets from people's past lives. Watches, rings, toasters, microwave ovens, musical instruments, all protected by rows of metal mesh gates. Jeebs, short and sleazy-looking, didn't care where the junk came from. He had a business to run.

"Officer Edwards!" said Jeebs, startled as Edwards walked up to the counter. "Oh, hey, how'd these get here? I thought I turned 'em in to the proper authorities."

He was talking about a box of about one hundred Rolex watches that he was appraising. He quickly slid them behind the counter.

"Way I hear it, Jeebs," said Edwards, "you're into something a little hotter than watches." He was doing his thing, putting pressure on the shop owner. He could feel Kay watching him from the shadows, judging his technique.

"Sure," Jeebs said with a laugh. "That's why I'm still here in the shop, 'cause I love the hours."

Edwards grabbed Jeebs by the collar. "I'm talking about guns, Jeebs," he said angrily. "High-tech stuff."

"C'mon, Edwards," replied Jeebs. "What you see is what I got."

"Why don't you show him the imports, Jeebs?" interjected Kay. He stepped forward, allowing the dull pawnshop light to fall across his face.

Jeebs recognized the man instantly. Edwards could see him become visibly unnerved.

"H-hiya, Kay," stuttered Jeebs to the man in black. "H-how are you?"

"The imports, Jeebs," Kay insisted. "Now."

"You know I got out of that business a long time ago, Kay," said Jeebs nervously.

"Why do you lie to me?" asked Kay. "I hate it when you lie to me." Kay pulled out a gun and aimed it at Jeebs's forehead. "I'm going to count to three . . ."

Edwards saw that Jeebs was shaking now. Whoever this Kay was, he was getting somewhere.

"He'll do it, Jeebs," said Edwards, playing along.

Kay began to count: "*One.*"

"I've *seen* him do it," added Edwards.

"*Two.*"

"Talk to me, Jeebs," said Edwards. "He's crazy when he's like this."

"He's always crazy," said Jeebs.

"*Three!*" said Kay. At that, he fired his gun, blowing Jeebs's head clear off.

Instinctively, Edwards pulled out his own gun and aimed it at Kay. He never dreamed Kay would actually pull the trigger. He had played that bad-cop-nice-cop game countless times before. Basic rule: You're not supposed to shoot a suspect's head off. Kay was obviously crazy.

"Put the gun down and put your hands on the counter!" Edwards ordered the man in black.

"I warned him," said Kay calmly.

"Drop the weapon!"

"You warned him."

"You are under arrest!" said Edwards. *"You have the right to remain silent!"*

"Don't do that," came a voice from behind the counter. "Did you know how much that hurt?"

Edwards whirled around and nearly dropped his gun, he was so startled. The voice belonged to Jeebs. Or, rather, to Jeebs's body. The body had risen from behind the counter. And much to Edwards's amazement, it was growing a brand-new head.

3.
The Neuralyzer

"**S**how us what you got," Kay said, aiming his gun at the newly resurrected shopkeeper. "Or I'll use up another one."

Jeebs nervously pressed a button on the underside of the counter. A mechanical whirr was heard and the counter opened, revealing a shelf piled high with unusual-looking weapons.

"Edwards?" asked Kay, pointing to the arsenal.

Edwards could barely move his eyes toward the counter. They were still firmly focused in Jeebs's direction.

"Edwards," repeated Kay. "Recognize any of these?"

Edwards glanced down at the counter. *Best to go along with all this,* he thought to himself. *Sort it out later.* The weapons were unusual all right. Most of them were just like the ones he saw the perp pull on him earlier that evening. Whatever they were, they weren't regular issue.

"Uh — this is what I saw," Edwards said, pointing to one of the weapons.

"You sold a carbonizer with implosion capacity to an unlicensed cephalopod?" Kay asked Jeebs angrily.

"He looked all right to me," replied Jeebs innocently.

"A carbonizer is an assassin's weapon, Jeebs," said Kay. "Who was the target?"

"I don't know," answered Jeebs.

Kay raised his gun again. "Jeebs . . ."

"*I don't know!*" insisted the shopkeeper.

Kay lowered his gun. "This is all confiscated," he said, pointing to the counter full of weapons. "All of it. I want you on the next transport off this rock."

Jeebs nodded, understanding. Kay turned and left.

Edwards was still shaken, but he tried not to show it. "Yeah," he warned Jeebs nervously. "And I'll be by tomorrow for those Rolexes." He staggered out of the shop in a daze.

"The eyelids, fine," Edwards said to Kay when he was outside. "And the jumping thing . . . and the gun, okay. But the head?"

Kay was standing coolly near the car. "Searching for a handle on the moment here?" he asked Edwards. "A place to file all this? Sorry, I can't help you, kid. Only comfort I can offer is that tomorrow you won't remember a thing."

"Oh, no," insisted Edwards. "*This* I'm gonna remember for a long, long time."

"Ever see one of these?" Edwards heard Kay ask. He looked down. Kay was holding a small metal tube. He dialed a setting on the device, aimed it at Edwards, and pressed a button.

Edwards never even remembered the blinding light that seared his eyes. All he knew was one minute he was chasing a half-crazed perp up Madison Avenue, the next minute he was sitting in a Chinese restaurant, looking down at a plate of beef and broccoli. He must have been in the restaurant for some time, because his food was nearly half-eaten.

And there was a voice coming at him from across the table. Loud. Rhythmic. Telling the tale end of a bad joke. "— and the wife says, 'Yeah, Harry, I know, but this one's eating my popcorn!'"

Edwards looked across the table. "Huh?" he said to the man across from him. The man was dressed entirely in black. The man looked vaguely familiar to Edwards, but where they had met he wasn't sure.

"Whoops, gotta run," said the man, checking his watch. He stood up and threw some money on the table. Among the bills was a small white business card. "You're a bright young man, James. I'll see you tomorrow, nine A.M. sharp."

The man turned and walked out of the restaurant.

Edwards weakly picked up the business card. On it was scribbled: *James D. Edwards, Saturday, 9 A.M., 504 Battery Drive.*

Edwards looked at the card, puzzled. He turned it over and looked at the other side. There wasn't much there. No name, no phone or fax number, no E-mail address. Just three little letters, dead in the middle of the card:

MiB

4.
The Farmer

Beatrice slaved all day over a hot stove just so her Edgar could have a nice hot meal when he came in from his day's work on the farm. Some weeks, when the profits were good, she was able to get something special from the market. Something that Edgar liked. Like a steak or a roast. Most days, however, the profits were bad. On those days the most she was able to afford was noodles and butter.

Today was a noodles and butter day. Her Edgar hated noodles and butter. And no sooner had he muddied the floor with his dirty work boots than he began telling her so.

"*I* go out," Edgar said, his eyes transfixed by the plate of slippery noodles Beatrice placed before him on the dining table. "*I* work my butt off to make a living, all I want is to come home to a nice clean house with a nice fat steak on the table, but instead I get this — this — I don't even know what you call this!"

27

Beatrice filled a plate of noodles of her own and sat down across from Edgar. She would let him rave on as she always did. No point in arguing about the noodles. It was all they could afford.

"I tell you what it *looks* like," continued Edgar as he played with the noodles with his fork. "It *looks* like poison."

Beatrice reached over for Edgar's plate. If he didn't like it, he didn't have to eat it. He slapped her hand away.

"Don't you take that away," he shouted. "I'm eatin' that. It *is* poison, isn't it? I swear, I wouldn't be surprised if it was, the way you skulk around here. You're useless, Beatrice, the only thing that pulls its weight around here is my truck!"

Just then a blast, some kind of explosion, came from outside. It was so powerful, the noodles nearly shook off their plates.

"Stay here!" Edgar ordered Beatrice. He leaped to his feet and threw open the door. Beatrice couldn't see what he saw, but she figured whatever it was must have been pretty awful. She saw Edgar take his twelve-gauge shotgun out of the closet and go outside.

After a few minutes Beatrice got up and went to the door. Edgar had gone out to the driveway. Only the driveway wasn't there anymore. Instead, there was a huge gaping hole the size of a small fishing pond in the ground.

"What is it, Edgar?" Beatrice called out.

"Get back in that house!" Edgar shouted.

Beatrice did as she was told. Edgar couldn't earn enough to eat anything better than boiled noodles, but he knew what was right. If he wanted Beatrice to remain in the house, then that was where she would remain.

Edgar stood in his driveway and stared at what was once his pickup truck, shocked. Now it was just an empty, hulking frame of scrap metal. Something, something powerful, had blown it to bits and replaced it with a deep, scorching hole.

And whatever that something was, it was in the hole. Edgar could feel it. Carefully, he aimed his twelve-gauge and peered down into the abyss. There was something down there, all right. Something hard and shiny.

"Place projectile weapon on the ground," came a hollow voice from the hole.

Edgar staggered back, terrified for a moment. Then he cocked his gun and approached the hole again. "You can have my gun when you pry it from my cold, dead fingers!" he shouted defiantly.

There was a momentary pause. Then: *"Your proposal is acceptable."*

As Edgar stared down into the hole in disbelief, a long, hairy tentacle, like something from a giant bug, popped out of the hole. It grabbed Edgar by the head and pulled him down.

*   *   *

Beatrice sat patiently at the dinner table, occasionally taking tiny bites out of one of the noodles on her plate. A few minutes later she heard footsteps. Edgar was coming back toward the house.

"What on earth was it?" asked Beatrice when Edgar took his place at the table.

"*Sugar*," replied Edgar. Only his voice was different. More refined.

"I've never seen sugar put a hole in a driveway before," said Beatrice, dumbfounded.

"*Give me sugar*," demanded Edgar. "*In water.*"

Suddenly Edgar frightened Beatrice. Something inside told her he had changed. It was almost as if he were a completely different person. Something else inside told her to do as he commanded. She went to the sink and mixed a glass of sugar water. She gave him the glass, her hand trembling.

Edgar took the glass and swallowed the sugar water in one motion. As he leaned back to swallow the drink, Beatrice noticed something odd about the skin on his neck.

"Edgar, your skin!" she exclaimed in terror. "It's — it's just *hanging* off your bones!"

Edgar slammed his glass on the table and looked at his reflection in the window. Then, as if he were adjusting a mask, he reached behind his head and pulled his skin back, tucking it into his shirt collar. Beatrice could see Edgar's whole face shift into place, like a rubber Halloween mask.

When Edgar was done, he turned to Beatrice and smiled. "That better?" he asked.

It was the last thing Beatrice heard before passing out in fright.

5.
The Recruit

Edwards couldn't figure it out. His memory of the previous evening was still a blank. Everything was gone except for that moment when he realized he was sitting in a Chinese restaurant. The card on the table had said MiB. There was an address on the other side. A man in black had given it to him.

Now it was the next morning. He arrived at the address, a rather ordinary-looking building downtown. A security guard let him into the building and directed him to the room he was in now. A man in black appeared, but there were also others in the room. Six others. Some in plain clothes, some uniformed.

"You're late," the man in black said to Edwards. "Sit down."

One chair was empty. He sat in it just as he was told.

"My name is Zed," said the man in black, addressing Edwards and the others. "You're all here because you're the best of the best. Marines, Navy SEALs, Army Rangers, Top Guns, NYPD. And we're looking for one of you. Just one. What will follow is a series of simple tests designed to quantify motor skills, hand-eye coordination, concentration, stamina. I see we have a question." Zed pointed to Edwards.

"I'm sorry," said Edwards as he lowered his hand. "It's just that no one really asked this, but — what exactly are we doing here?"

Another recruit raised his hand. Crew cut shaved close. Probably army. Zed called on him.

"Jake Jensen, West Point graduate with honors," said the cadet in a loud and formal tone of voice. Then he answered the question. "We're here because you're looking for the best of the best, *sir*!"

Edwards laughed.

"What's so funny, Edwards?" asked Zed.

"I — I don't know, sir," Edwards said, trying not to laugh. He pointed at the cadet. "This guy. 'Best of the best of the best —.' It struck me as — humorous."

Nobody else was laughing. Everyone remained quiet until Edwards finally stopped.

"Okay," said Zed flatly. "Let's get started."

A written exam was passed out to the men. It was several pages long. Edwards looked it over. Some math, some history, some diagrams.

Still, he and the others plowed through pages,

filling in the blank spaces with pencils that were provided for them. There were no desks in the room, so the men struggled to fill in the answers on their laps.

It wasn't easy. More than one guy ripped through the pages with his pencil.

Edwards looked around. There was a table on the other side of the room. Might as well use it, no one else was. He got up, dragged the table over to his seat, then sat back down and continued writing, this time using the table as a desk. That was better.

When the recruits had finished the written exam, they were led into another room. A bunch of weapons sat on a table in front of them. Across the room was a blank wall.

"Any of you guys know what we're doing here?" Edwards asked the others.

"Looking for the best of the best of the best," replied the cadet.

Edwards couldn't help but grin at the brilliant answer. "Yeah, I know, but —"

Just then the far wall pulled apart. The whole room began to pulsate with multicolored lights. From out of nowhere three flying images, two otherworldly and one human, soared around them. The recruits knew at once they were under a simulated attack.

Instinctively, each recruit reached for a weapon, took aim, and fired at an image. While the others shot several blasts at the alien creatures, Edwards hesitated briefly, then fired at the one creature who was obviously human — a little girl. And he got it with a single shot to the head.

Then a door opened and Zed entered the room. He walked straight to Edwards.

"May I ask why you felt little Tiffany deserved to die?" asked Zed.

"She was the only one who actually looked dangerous to me," replied Edwards. "At the time."

"And how did you come to that conclusion?"

"Hook-headed guy," said Edwards, pointing to the frozen image of an alien simulation. "You explain to me how he can think with a hook for a head. Answer: It's not his head. His head is that ugly beanbag thing over there. And if you look at the snarling beast-guy, he's not snarling, he's sneezing — he's got tissues in his hand. Where I'm looking, the little girl was the only one who appeared to have a motive. Do I owe her an apology?"

Zed stepped back out and began having a debate with another man in black. Through the doorway Edwards could see that the other man was the man from the Chinese restaurant. He had an idea that any second now he would find out what all this was about.

"Congratulations," Zed told the recruits as he came back into the shooting gallery. "You're everything we've come to expect from years of government training. Now, if you'll just follow me, we have one more test to administer. An eye exam."

The recruits followed Zed out into the hall. Edwards was the last to go. As soon as he stepped outside the room, he approached the man from the Chinese restaurant.

"You," said Edwards to the man in black. "What's going on? Who are you guys?"

The man in black didn't answer. Instead, he motioned for Edwards to follow him down the hall.

"Call me Kay, kid," began the man. "Back in the mid-fifties, the government started a little under-funded agency with the simple and laughable purpose of making contact with a race not of this planet."

They had reached an alcove. Edwards saw the other recruits. Zed was standing in front of them holding a small metal tube. Zed pressed a button on the tube and a blinding flash of white light went off. The recruits became dazed and disoriented. They were led away.

Edwards realized he had seen that flash of light before — but where?

Kay handed Edwards a file stuffed thick with photographs. Edwards riffled through them. The shots were more than thirty years old. And they were weird. Men in black suits in old offices. Spaceships hovering in the night sky. Kay as a much younger man holding out a bouquet of flowers.

"Everybody thought the agency was a joke, except the aliens," continued Kay. "They made contact on March 2, 1961, just outside New York City. I was just a kid. That night I got lost on the wrong back road."

"You brought the aliens flowers?" Edwards asked.

"Son, they were intergalactic refugees with a simple request," explained Kay. "Let us use Earth as an apolitical zone for people without a planet. Ever see the movie *Casablanca*? Same thing, except no Nazis. We agreed. So we masked all evidence of their landing."

Edwards was looking at another picture now. It was the 1964 World's Fair, still under construction. Giant models of rockets marked the fair's theme of space travel. There were two towers, each with a flying saucer mounted at its top.

"The 1964 World's Fair was a cover-up?" asked Edwards in amazement.

"Why else would we hold it in Queens?" answered Kay. He led Edwards down another corridor. "More nonhumans arrive every year. They live among us, in secret."

"I see," said Edwards looking at Kay as if he were crazy. "Not to change the subject, but when was your last CAT scan?"

"Every six months, sport," replied Kay with frankness. "It's company policy."

Edwards handed Kay back the file of photos.

"Well, thanks for the very amusing morning," he said politely. "But I'm hopin' you'll show me where I came in? 'Cause this is where I go out."

"Sure, kid," said Kay with a smile. "Hang on, I wanna grab a cup of coffee." He opened a door and motioned for Edwards to follow him into a kitchenette.

Edwards walked into the room and immediately his jaw dropped. Standing around the small kitchen were four wormlike creatures. The tiny, thin things were holding a conversation in a language that sounded like a weak signal on a car radio.

Edwards realized that the creatures were definitely not of this Earth.

"How's it going, guys?" Kay asked the creatures as he poured himself a cup of coffee. The aliens screeched their answers.

"Don't tell me we've only got this powdered cream again," complained Kay as he picked up a jar of DairyMate. One of the creatures hissed and pointed to the counter.

"Oh." Kay nodded when he saw the container of real cream. "Thanks."

Edwards studied the aliens in amazement as Kay poured the cream into his coffee. Everything Kay had been telling him was the truth!

And there was more. Kay led Edwards outside. While Kay drank his coffee, Edwards tried to make sense of it all.

"Any given time," explained Kay, "around fif-

38

teen-hundred landed aliens are on the planet, the majority right here in Manhattan. They do their best to look like us when they're in public. Some of them are better than others. Most aliens are decent enough, just trying to make a living."

"Cabdrivers?" asked Edwards. He always thought cabbies were a little weird.

"Not as many as you'd think, son," replied Kay. "Humans, for the most part, don't have a clue. Don't want one either. They're happy. They think they got a pretty good bead on things."

"Why the big secret?" asked Edwards. "People are smart. They can handle it."

"A *person* is smart, son," replied Kay. "*People* are dumb. Everything they've ever known has been proven to be wrong. A thousand years ago everybody *knew* as a fact that Earth was the center of the universe. Five hundred years ago they *knew* it was flat. Fifteen minutes ago you knew we humans were alone on it. Imagine what you'll know tomorrow."

Edwards paused, trying to take it all in. He knew what they wanted of him now. It was clear. They needed a new recruit for their organization. He was the best candidate for the job. After all, he was the only one in the testing room to realize an unused table was in the room. That made him "the best of the best of the best," didn't it? It was as if he were being called upon not just to serve his country, but the whole world. The universe, even.

He began to wonder what he would look like dressed in black.

"So what's the catch?" he asked Kay.

"Son, what you gain in perspective, you'll lose in ways you're too young to understand. You give up everything," replied Kay. "No one will know you exist. Ever."

"Nobody?"

"You're not even allowed a favorite shirt. There. That's the speech they never gave me, kid. The choice I never got."

Why was Kay making it sound so negative? "Hold up," said Edwards. "You track me down, put me through those dumb tests, now you're trying to talk me out of it. I don't get it."

"You have until sunup to decide," said Kay, finishing his coffee.

"Is it worth it?" asked Edwards.

Kay stood up. "Yeah. If you're strong enough," he said. And with that he walked away, leaving Edwards to ponder his future.

Edwards sat on the bench, alone, for the rest of the day. He could hardly believe what had happened that morning, what Kay had told him, that he had actually seen aliens from other planets. When he finally looked up at the sky, twilight was approaching. There seemed to be more stars in the sky than he had ever noticed before. The heavens seemed vast and endless.

6.
The Exterminator

Edgar never went to bed that night. Instead, he sat at the dining table, adjusting and readjusting his head. He had to get it just right. The head was uncomfortable, but he knew he wouldn't be able to move among the humans without it.

Just after dawn, Edgar heard a van grind its way up the road and then turn into the driveway. It stopped at the garage. Edgar went out to investigate. A huge cockroach was painted on the side of the van. A man got out carrying a tank and hose.

Edgar smiled. The van was big enough. He walked over to the garage. The man with the tank was aiming his hose at a cluster of spiders that were crawling everywhere.

"Got a little eviction notice for you, boys," the man told the bugs as he prepared to spray them with toxic gas from the tank.

"Just what exactly do you think you're doing?"

asked Edgar when he saw what the man was going to do.

"Hello, Edgar," said the man. "It's that time of the month again. Just takin' care of your pest problem."

"Pest problem?" asked Edgar, insulted at the word. *"Pest?"*

"Yeah," replied the exterminator. "You've got a *big* infestation problem."

"You know, I *have* noticed an infestation here," said Edgar. "Everywhere I look, in fact. Nothing but undeveloped, unevolved, barely conscious pond scum. So convinced of their own superiority, they scurry about their short, pointless lives."

The exterminator looked at the spiders crawling along the rafters of the garage. "Yeah," he agreed. "Don't you want to get rid of them?"

"In the worst way," said Edgar. And with that he lashed out quickly, doing away with the exterminator. Then he climbed into the exterminator's van and drove it over to the great pit that was still in the driveway. He opened the van's rear doors. Next he raised one end of a sheet of plywood on the back of the van to form a ramp.

Then he jumped into the pit.

His spaceship was no longer hot. It had been cooled by the mud and dirt that surrounded it. Edgar reached under the ship and, grunting with effort, slowly pushed the ship out of the pit, up the ramp, and onto the back of the exterminator's van.

Edgar smiled with satisfaction. That was easy enough.

He adjusted his head again, climbed into the van, and drove off. He had already decided on where to begin his mission.

7.
Jay

"**O**ne thing you gotta know right now," Edwards told Kay as they stood at the entrance of the MiB building. Before he took the job, there were a couple of little things he wanted to get straight. He thought of them as personality problems.

"Go ahead, kid," said Kay.

"All right," Edwards started. "You chose me 'cause you recognize my skills. So as of now you can cease with all of that calling me 'son' or 'kid' or 'sport.' Cool?"

"Whatever you say, slick," quipped Kay. "Now, about your skills, as of this moment they don't mean too much. You're not dealing with people."

And with that Kay led Edwards into a vast room. It was a huge, multileveled workplace of steel and glass. Humans and aliens were everywhere, working side by side. Kay led Edwards onto a platform where a long line of aliens, many carrying luggage, were showing their immigration documents to an official-looking human customs agent.

"Purpose of trip?" the agent asked the next alien in line.

"Diplomatic mission," replied the alien, a large humanoid visitor with a pale face.

"Duration of stay?" asked the agent.

"Lunch," replied the alien.

Edwards kept staring, fascinated by the scene, until Kay hurried him along.

"What branch of the government do we report to?" Edwards asked Kay.

"None. They started asking too many questions."

"So who pays for all this?"

"We sold a few patents on gadgets we confiscated from our out-of-state visitors," explained Kay. "Velcro. Microwave ovens. Liposuction. They're all ours."

Kay led Edwards across the room until they reached a giant video screen. Zed stood beside it.

"Observation," explained Kay, indicating the screen. "The heart of our little endeavor."

The screen displayed a map of the world with thousands of tiny lights blinking in all parts of the globe. Data flashed near each tiny light at lightning speed.

"This map shows the location of every registered alien on Earth at any given time," Kay continued to explain. "Some of them we keep under

45

constant surveillance. Everyone on these screens is an alien. In public they look normal. In private — you get the idea."

On the screen flashed several aliens who were living on Earth disguised as humans.

"I gotta be honest about something," said Edwards.

"It makes no sense?" Kay anticipated.

"It makes perfect sense," replied Edwards. "When I was a third-grader in Philadelphia, they told me I was crazy 'cause I swore that our teacher was from, like, Venus or something."

"Ah, yes," said Kay. "Mrs. Edelson."

Edwards looked at the screen, stunned. Mrs. Edelson's face appeared. "She was from Jupiter, actually," said Kay.

Zed faced Edwards. "Let's put it on."

"Put what on?" asked Edwards.

"The last suit you'll ever wear."

Edwards followed Kay and Zed into a locker room. The room was all white. White walls, white floor, white ceiling, white lockers.

Zed opened a locker and pulled out a black suit, forty regular. He told Edwards to put it on.

"From now on you'll dress only in attire specially sanctioned by MiB Special Services," explained Zed as Edwards put on his new clothes. "You'll conform to the identity we give you, eat where we tell you, live where we tell you, get approval for any expenditure over a hundred dollars."

When Edwards had the suit on, the Men in Black led him to a booth. Inside, Edwards placed his fingers on a globe with ten glowing red spots. A laser beam removed Edwards's fingerprints from his fingers.

"You will have no identifying marks of any kind," said Zed as Edwards waited for the slightly painful procedure to be over. "You will not stand out in any way. Your entire image is carefully crafted to leave no lasting memory whatsoever with anyone you encounter. You're a rumor, recognizable only as a *déjà vu*, and dismissed just as quickly."

Edwards put on a pair of shiny black shoes.

"You don't exist," continued Zed. "You were never even born. Anonymity is your name. Silence your native tongue."

Edwards slipped on a pair of black sunglasses.

"You are no longer part of the system. You are above the system."

Edwards adjusted his belt and tie. He followed Zed and Kay out of the locker room and over to a computer. A name appeared on the screen in front of him. It was his own name. James Darrel Edwards III. One by one the computer deleted the letters of Edwards's name until nothing was left but the "J."

"From this day on you will be referred to only by the letter 'J.' We're 'them.' We're 'they.'"

Edwards looked down at a monogram on his new crisp shirt cuff. *J.*

"We are the Men in Black."

8.
Birth of an Alien

Jay was taken to Zed's office, a circular, windowed room that looked over the main MiB complex. Lined along the walls were several video monitors each with a feed from a different part of the world. On each monitor was another man in black.

"Okay, let's see," said Zed as he shuffled through some paperwork on his desk. "Bee, we got the deposed sur-prefect of Sinalee touching down in the forest outside Portland tonight. I'm pulling you down from Anchorage to do a meet and greet."

"Humanoid?" asked Bee, a man on one of the monitors.

"You wish," answered Zed. "Bring a sponge."

Zed turned a page on his desk. "Let's see. What else? Red-letter from last night. We had an unauthorized landing somewhere in upstate New York farm country. Keep your ears open for this one, Kay. We're not hosting an intergalactic party here."

Just then Zed's computer screen began to beep urgently.

"Well, well," said Zed as he watched the report coming over the screen. "We got a skimmer."

Jay looked at Kay, confused.

"Landed alien out of zone," explained Kay. "Who is it?"

"Redgick," replied Zed. "He's not cleared to leave Manhattan, but he's *way* out of town now, stuck in traffic on the New Jersey Turnpike. Why don't you take Jay. This is a good one for him to warm up on."

Jay followed Kay outside, where a black LTD was waiting for them. It was an '86 and it looked it.

"We got the use of unlimited technology from the entire universe and we cruise around in *this*?" asked Jay as he climbed into the car.

Kay grunted with annoyance and slammed his door. He started the car. It hummed, not like the usual Ford, but like a Stealth airplane.

"Seat belt," ordered Kay.

Jay hesitated. "You know," he began, "y'all gotta learn to talk to people. You could be a little kinder and gentler."

"Buckle up, *please*," said Kay, gritting his teeth.

Jay did so. "Now did that hurt?" he asked sheepishly.

Kay ignored Jay and shifted the car into reverse. Suddenly the power of the car was awesome. Jay sailed forward, hitting the dashboard. When Kay shifted into forward, Jay slammed back into his seat.

A lighted panel rotated into place between the two front seats. Jay's hand nearly fell on a flashing red button at the top of the panel. Kay brushed his hand away.

"Jay, the button," said Kay.

"What about it?" asked Jay.

"*Never* push the button, Jay."

Jay sighed as the car took off down the road at breakneck speed. He was surprised at the smoothness of the ride. They had souped up this hot rod good. Real good.

Kay drove quickly up the West Side Highway, then through the tunnel and onto the turnpike. It wasn't long before he spotted the car he was looking for and pulled it over.

Jay followed Kay as they walked over to the stopped car. Behind the wheel was a man in his mid-thirties. In the backseat was a woman. And she was pregnant.

"License and registration, please," Kay demanded from the driver. The driver handed over some documents. Kay flipped through them. Standard New York papers in perfect order. He handed them back.

"Now your *other* license and registration, please, Mr. Redgick," said Kay.

The man paused. Then he reached into his pocket and handed over two cards. The cards were marked *Resident Alien ID*. On the cards were photographs of two aquatic-looking types, husband and wife, smiling at the camera, their long, skinny, pointed tongues dangling in a friendly way.

Jay looked at Mr. Redgick and his wife again. He was looking for a sign. Any sign. No way. They looked like a perfectly human couple to him.

Kay handed the cards back to the driver. "Your resident card has you restricted to the five boroughs only. Where do you think you're going?"

"It's my wife," Mr. Redgick said, starting to panic. "She's — she's — well, *look*!"

Kay and Jay peered into the backseat. Mrs. Redgick was obviously going to have a baby, and soon.

Kay straightened up, fast. "How soon?" he asked the driver.

The woman screamed in pain. An answer to Kay's question: *real* soon.

"Okay, all right. No big deal," said Kay. He turned to Jay and said: "You handle it."

"Me?" Jay was stunned.

"Sure," said Kay. "It's easy."

A look of stark terror crossed Jay's face as he climbed into the car beside Mrs. Redgick.

"Are you sure he knows what he's doing?" he heard Mr. Redgick ask Kay.

"Yeah, sure," Kay replied. "He does this all the

time. C'mon, let him work, Redgick. There're a few things I wanna ask you."

Kay led Mr. Redgick a few yards away from the car.

"Croagg the midwife's back on Sixty-fourth and Eighth," he told the alien. "You were headed *out* of town."

Redgick looked at the ground nervously. "Well," he stammered, "we're, uh — meeting someone."

"So, who you meeting?" asked Kay suspiciously.

"Well, it's — a ship," replied Redgick.

"Really?" Kay asked doubtfully. "I didn't see a departure clearance for today."

Redgick shuffled uncomfortably. "You didn't?" he asked. "Uh — well, it was an emergency."

"What kind of emergency? What's the rush to get off the planet all of a sudden?"

"We just don't like the neighborhood anymore," answered Redgick. "Some of the — new arrivals."

"What new arrivals?" probed Kay. Redgick was clearly concealing something from him. "This have anything to do with the crasher from last night?"

"Help. *Help!* Hellooo!" Jay interrupted from the back of the car. "Can you guys talk later?"

Kay approached the car just as Jay came flying out, clutching the alien baby to his chest. Jay had done it. Mr. Redgick was a father!

"Congratulations!" Kay said, slapping Redgick on the back. "It's a squid!"

Mr. Redgick ran to see if his wife was all right.

She was. In a few minutes Kay allowed the Redgicks, united with their newborn, to drive away. Then he motioned Jay back toward the LTD.

"Anything about that seem unusual to you?" asked Kay.

Dumb question. "Pick," replied Jay, wiping baby alien vomit off his suit.

Kay sighed. "What kind of 'new arrival' would scare Redgick so that he'd risk a warp jump with a newborn?"

Jay stared blankly at Kay. He had no idea.

Kay started up the car. "Something's up," he said. "Let's check the hot sheets." He headed the LTD back toward the city.

When they reached midtown, Kay pulled to a stop at a corner newsstand. Seconds later he returned with a copy of the latest scandal sheet. The headline was typical: *Man Eats Own House.*

"*This* is what you call a hot sheet?" asked Jay, dumbstruck.

"Best investigative reporting on the planet," replied Kay as he thumbed through the tabloid newspaper's pages.

"You're actually looking for leads in a supermarket tabloid?"

"Not looking for. *Found.*" replied Kay. Then he showed Jay a page with the headline: *Farm Wife Says "Alien Stole My Husband's Skin!"*

9.
The Farmer's Wife

Peaceful countryside usually made Jay restless. He preferred the beat of the city, the language of the streets. It was where he felt most comfortable.

That was then. Now, as Kay drove the LTD northward toward New York State farm country, Jay felt glad to leave the urban congestion behind. Even if it was just for a few hours.

He had to think. To make some sense of it all. Somehow the serenity of the passing country landscape helped him to do so.

Reality check. He was a cop. That hadn't changed. Act like one. Protect the public from the perps. It's just that the perps have tentacles now. And they fly around in spaceships. And a lady a few miles up the road says her husband was killed by an alien who stole his skin.

Reality check. That's some reality.

"Can I help you gentlemen?" said the farmer's wife, introducing herself as Beatrice. She had come out of the house to meet them.

Kay pulled the LTD to a stop in the driveway. He couldn't go any farther. A huge pit stood between the driveway and the house.

"How do you do, ma'am," said Kay as he and Jay got out of the car. "I'm Special Agent Manheim and this is Agent Black, FBI. Had a few questions about your visitor."

"Are you here to make fun of me, too?" asked Beatrice.

"No, ma'am," replied Kay. "We at the FBI don't have a sense of humor that we're aware of. Okay if we come in?"

"Sure," replied Beatrice. "Lemonade?"

No sooner had Jay and Kay followed the woman into her kitchen than she poured them some lemonade and began telling her story. It happened a few days ago. Edgar had come in from the farm, tired from his daily chores. They had noodles and butter sauce that night. Then they heard the explosion. Edgar got his gun and went out to investigate. There was a hole in the ground where the driveway used to be. Edgar came back.

He was different.

She called the sheriff. Then came the reporters.

"And *they* said to me," continued Beatrice, "'If he was murdered, how could he walk back in the house?' And I must admit, I was a little stumped by that one. But I know Edgar. And that wasn't him. It was more like something *else* that was *wearing* him. Like a suit. An Edgar suit."

Jay caught sight of a photo on the mantelpiece. Edgar. Ugly as a human, must be a gross-out as an alien. Now what the farm lady was saying made a little sense. What she was saying — and what Kay seemed to already know — was that her husband's body was taken over by some mysterious arrival from space. An arrival so terrifying, it frightened good, law-abiding aliens like the Redgicks into fleeing the planet.

"Anyway," continued the farmer's wife, "when I came to, he was gone."

"Did he say anything?" asked Kay.

"Yes," Beatrice remembered. "He asked for water. Sugar water."

"Sugar water," said Kay.

Jay pointed to his glass. "Did you taste her lemonade?"

Kay nodded. He put on his sunglasses and drew his neuralyzer. Jay took out his sunglasses, too. Poor woman. After the blinding flash, she sat dazed.

"Okay, Beatrice," Kay said to the groggy woman. "There was no alien, and the flash of light you saw in the sky wasn't a UFO. Swamp gas from a weather balloon was trapped in a thermal pocket and refracted the light from Venus —"

"Whoa!" interjected Jay. "That thing erases her memory and you give her a new one?"

"Standard issue neuralyzer," replied Kay.

"And that's the best you can come up with?"

Kay turned back to Beatrice. "On a more personal note, Beatrice," he continued, "Edgar ran off with an old girlfriend. Go stay at your mother's for a few days and get over it. Decide you're better off."

"Yeah," added Jay. "And you're better off because he never appreciated you anyway. In fact, you *kicked* him out, and now that he's gone, you ought to buy some new clothes, maybe hire a decorator or something."

When Beatrice's mind was completely replaced with new memories, Jay followed Kay back out to the pit in the driveway.

Kay had taken out a small, box-shaped device and was scanning the pit.

"Hey, Kay," said Jay. "When am I gonna get one of those memory things?"

"When you're ready," replied Kay. He was watching his scanner. Colors were changing from red to yellow. "Please, not green," he muttered. Yellow to purple.

It turned green.

"Do you know what alien life-form leaves a green spectral trail?" Kay asked Jay.

"Wait, don't tell me. That was the question on final *Jeopardy* last night, right?" Jay responded.

Kay turned off his analyzer and sighed softly. "We have a Bug," he said.

Jay didn't like the sound of that. "I'm gonna

"We're above the system. Over it. Beyond it. We are the Men in Black."

"Hand me your head and put up your arms."

"Only comfort I can offer is that tomorrow you won't remember a thing." Kay uses his neuralyzer on Edwards to erase his memory of the aliens.

"Edgar, your skin!" Beatrice exclaims. "It's hanging off of your bones!" Edgar reaches behind his head and pulls his skin back, tucking it into his shirt collar.

Kay leads Edwards into MiB headquarters —
humans and aliens are everywhere.

"Back in the mid-fifties,
the government started a
little underfunded agency
with the simple and laughable purpose of making
contact with a race not
of this planet. Everybody
thought the agency was a
joke," Kay tells Edwards.
"Except the aliens."

"The aliens made contact on March 2, 1961, just outside New York City."

"More nonhumans arrive every year. They live among us, in secret."

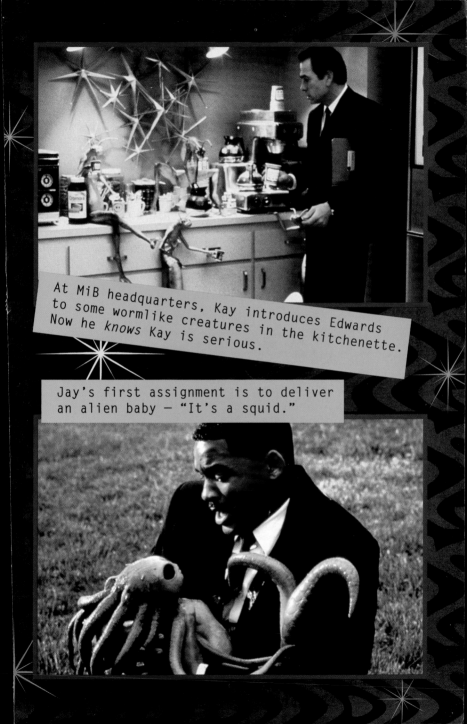

At MiB headquarters, Kay introduces Edwards to some wormlike creatures in the kitchenette. Now he *knows* Kay is serious.

Jay's first assignment is to deliver an alien baby — "It's a squid."

"You can kill us both," Rosenberg tells Edgar. "But it will not stop the peace."

Jay and Dr. Laurel Weaver, the morgue medical examiner, find that Rosenberg's head opens up to reveal . . .

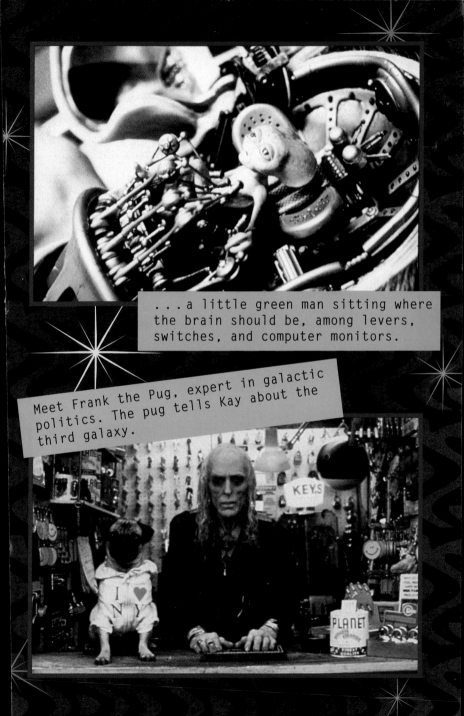

...a little green man sitting where the brain should be, among levers, switches, and computer monitors.

Meet Frank the Pug, expert in galactic politics. The pug tells Kay about the third galaxy.

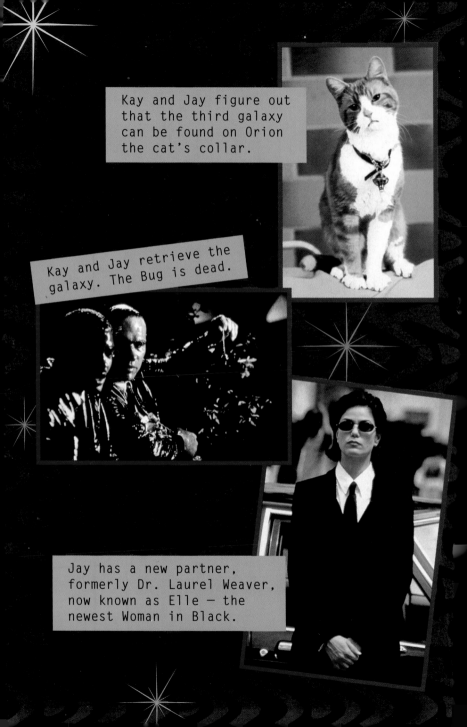

Kay and Jay figure out that the third galaxy can be found on Orion the cat's collar.

Kay and Jay retrieve the galaxy. The Bug is dead.

Jay has a new partner, formerly Dr. Laurel Weaver, now known as Elle — the newest Woman in Black.

jump way past you and just guess that this is bad," he said. "Right?"

"Bugs thrive on carnage, tiger," replied Kay. "They consume, infest, destroy. They live off the death and decay of other species."

"So basically you have a racial problem with all insect-based life-forms?"

"Listen, kid," said Kay. "Imagine a giant cockroach five times smarter than Albert Einstein, four times stronger than an ox, nine times meaner than an angry pit bull, strutting his stuff around Manhattan Island in his brand-new Edgar suit. Does that sound like fun?"

"What do we do?" asked Jay.

"With a Bug in town?" asked Kay. "We watch the morgues."

10.
Summit

Rosenberg looked at his watch. It was time and he didn't want to be late. Not for something this important.

He put a sign in the window. *Closed.* Come back tomorrow for your diamond bracelets, wedding rings, and watch batteries. He put on his coat and hat. He tucked the ornate jewelry box under one arm. He picked up his cat with the other.

He locked up. Five locks in all. Scary business, jewelry.

But it paled in comparison to today's other business. He could fall behind in repairing old Mrs. Weintraub's family heirlooms, but he couldn't be late today. If he was, he knew, there might not be any tomorrow.

Dusk was falling. The streets were mostly empty now except for a few ominous dark shadows. He walked hurriedly along the pale gray city streets, his arms still encumbered by the jewelry box and the cat.

What was that? Something coming up from behind! Rosenberg glanced over his shoulder. Then he relaxed. It was nothing. Just a van. A pest exterminator. Relax, relax. Nothing will ruin tonight. Everything will go just as planned.

Finally, he reached the little Russian diner where the meeting was scheduled to take place.

Inside, the Arquillian — the alien on a diplomatic mission — was waiting for him. He stood and embraced Rosenberg.

Rosenberg placed the jewelry box between them on the table. The cat sat quietly rolled up on top of it.

A tear fell down Rosenberg's face. He wiped it away, embarrassed.

"I'm sorry," apologized Rosenberg. "I was thinking of all the lives laid down in hopes that this day might eventually arrive."

"To peace," said the Arquillian, pouring Rosenberg a drink. The two drank to the sentiment.

"And to think that after so long, we should come together on a tiny little pebble like this," laughed the Arquillian.

"Earth?" replied Rosenberg. "It's not so bad once you get used to the smell."

The Arquillian set down his glass. It was time for business. "All right," he said. "Where is it?"

Rosenberg petted his cat. "Please," he said, soothed by the animal's purr. "You've waited this long, at least let me eat."

The Arquillian relaxed. "Of course," he said, smiling with confidence. "Why not? After eons of fighting, what's another fifteen minutes? Enjoy!"

The Arquillian called a waiter over and Rosenberg ordered. Pierogis. A small portion.

Rosenberg and the Arquillian continued to toast each other as they waited for the food.

"To the return of the Third Galaxy," toasted the Arquillian. "To Arquillian rule."

After a short time the waiter returned and placed a plate of pierogis on the table. This was followed by an enormous silverfish bug that crawled out from under the waiter's sleeve. Soon a whole horde of bugs was crawling all over the table.

Rosenberg looked up at the waiter and dropped his glass in fright. It wasn't the same man who had taken his order. He had seen this new waiter's face somewhere before. Where? Then he remembered: the newspaper. The photograph of the farmer, the one called Edgar.

The Arquillian recognized Edgar as well.

"You can kill us both," Rosenberg told Edgar. "But it will not stop the peace."

Edgar smiled. Rosenberg was right about one thing. A long stinger shot out from under Edgar's apron and zipped under the table. It pierced both Rosenberg's and the Arquillian's bellies at the same time. They winced with pain. They lurched forward.

Rosenberg watched helplessly as Edgar shoved

the cat out of the way, placed the jewelry box under his arm, and ran out of the restaurant.

Rosenberg could tell at once that the Arquillian was dead. In a few moments, he knew, he would also be dead. He spent his last few seconds listening to his cat, which still sat on the table, purring away.

11.
The Prince of Balta

Jay stared at the pretty medical examiner. Dr. Laurel Weaver had fallen asleep at her desk in the city morgue. Maybe she reasoned that she must have been asleep all along. That it was some kind of crazy dream that homicide had brought the bodies of two old men and one young waiter who had been murdered in a Russian diner. A dream that she stood hunched over the bodies and made the incisions, thus getting a head start on her next day's work.

A dream that what she found inside two of the bodies wasn't human. It was like nothing she had ever seen in her biology classes.

Jay watched as she slowly woke up and saw the cat, and probably realized it wasn't a dream at all. One of the dead men had a cat with him when he died. Maybe the detectives thought they were being funny, but they brought the cat to the morgue along with the bodies. It sat on the desk next to Laurel, watching her every move.

"Are you having a bad day, baby?" Laurel asked the animal, stroking its soft fur. Then she looked over at the old man's body, still laid out on the examining table, and added: "Don't worry. *His* is worse."

Laurel clicked on a small tape recorder, the one she must have been speaking into before she fell asleep.

"— approximately one hundred and twelve degrees at time of autopsy, indicating, quite possibly, an *increase* in body temperature after death," she said, reading from her notes. "This can be described only as really —"

"Weird?" Kay finished for her.

Laurel spun around. Jay watched her for a sign, any sign that she knew who he was. He knew at once that Kay and the others had done a thorough job with him. He must have looked only vaguely familiar to Laurel. It was clear she couldn't place him. It was as if he were a memory she knew she had, but had long ago forgotten.

Kay stepped forward and held out a card that read *Department of Public Health.* "I'm Dr. Leo Menville, Department of Public Health. This is Dr. White."

Jay nodded hello.

"You got something unusual?" Kay asked Laurel.

She nodded and walked over to the dead bodies. "The first corpse was perfectly normal," she began, indicating the corpse of the young waiter.

"But when I opened up the other two — well, look."

She threw back a sheet and exposed the bodies of the two old men.

"There's a skeletal structure at work here unlike anything I've ever seen," she explained.

Kay stepped closer to the larger of the bodies, the Arquillian. "I'll have a look at this one," he said. "Dr. White, why don't you and Dr. Weaver check out the other body?"

Jay hesitated. Autopsy was not his area. But Kay was serious. There was work to be done. He followed Dr. Weaver across the room to the other gurney.

"This one's even stranger," said Laurel as she and Jay stood overlooking the corpse. "I started with the lesser curvature of the stomach. Though, if you want we could begin at the gastro-esophageal junction."

Jay swallowed. Hard. "I think we should start at the same place you did," he said. Just then the cat meowed. "Your cat?" asked Jay.

"Guess it is now," replied Laurel. "Came in with the bodies."

She handed Jay a pair of rubber gloves. Then she snapped on a pair and began the procedure.

"Okay," she said to Jay.

Jay reluctantly reached into the body. Dr. Weaver helped him, guiding him through the examination.

"You know, you have very pretty eyes," she told Jay suddenly.

Jay blushed. "Thank you," he replied.

Laurel smiled. "Feel that? Where the pyloric junction would be?"

Jay didn't feel anything familiar. In fact, he had no idea what he was doing. "Oh, yes," he said, lying. "Exactly."

"Now, push that aside. Notice anything strange? Stomach? Liver? Lungs?"

Jay fished around, hoping to look like he knew what he was doing. "Nope," he said. "All fine."

Laurel paused. Something was wrong with the answer. "Doctor," she said. "They're all missing."

"Well, of course they are," shot back Jay quickly, covering up his blunder. "What I'm pointing out is that there are no pieces of them left. So they're intact, wherever they are. That we can be sure of."

Laurel gave Jay a long look. "Have we met before?" she asked. "I have the strangest feeling of *déjà vu.*"

"You know, I was going to ask you the same thing."

Laurel looked skeptically at Jay. "You know what I really think?" she asked. Jay shook his head. "But don't tell your partner. He looks like he's under enough stress already. I think this body is not really a body, but it's actually some sort of transport unit for something else altogether. The question is, what?"

Jay stared at Dr. Weaver. Not only was she beautiful, but she was smart.

Just then they heard Kay clearing his throat from the other side of the room. Jay walked over to him, but his concentration was still on Dr. Weaver.

"What do you think?" he asked Jay.

"*Very* interesting," Jay replied, his stare focused on the pretty medical examiner.

"Of the *body*," insisted Kay.

Jay jumped back to reality. "Not a clue," he admitted.

"All right," said Kay. "Keep her occupied. And try not to sound too dumb."

"Dr. White," Dr. Weaver called him from across the room. Jay didn't react, not recognizing his code name.

"Dr. *White!*" Laurel called again, this time shouting. "Look at this."

"You're up, slugger," Kay said, nudging Jay. Jay walked back to Laurel. She was pointing at some strange stitching around the ear of the dead man.

"What is that?" asked Jay. He reached out and touched the ear. It opened like a latch. Next he heard a mechanical hum come from inside the corpse's head. Then the head began to push out. A second later, the dead man's face popped open like a vault door.

Inside the head, where a skull should be, was a

tiny control room complete with levers, switches, computer, and video monitors. Sitting in a tiny little chair in front of a tiny little control console was a tiny little green man.

Jay and Laurel stared at the little man in astonishment.

"*Must* —" the little man was saying. He seemed dazed. "*Must — to pre — pre-vent — contest? No — to prevent —*"

"It's okay," Jay said, trying to calm him. "What are you trying to say? 'Struggle'?"

"'War'?" asked Laurel.

The little man nodded vigorously. "*Yes!*" he said. "*Galaxy on — or — or — Orion's — What is word? — Be — be —*"

"'Bed'?" asked Jay. "'Belt'? 'Orion's Belt'?"

The little green man nodded again. Then grabbed his chest and collapsed. Dead.

Jay and Laurel looked at each other, dumbfounded.

"'To prevent war, the galaxy is on Orion's Belt?'" said Jay, repeating what the little green man had seemed to say. "What does that mean?"

He called Kay over. Kay immediately began to examine the little green man.

"You guys are not with the Department of Public Health, are you?" asked Laurel.

Jay shook his head. "Is he dead?" he asked Kay.

Kay nodded. "Rosenberg," he said. "Good man."

"You knew the little green guy?" asked Jay.

"One of the few I actually liked," replied Kay. "Exiled high prince."

"I was right," interjected Laurel. "This is an alien life-form and you're from some government agency who wants to keep it under wraps."

Kay and Jay ignored her.

"He said, 'To prevent war, the galaxy is on Orion's Belt,'" Jay told Kay.

"This makes total sense," Laurel went on. "The other night I'm in a cab, this guy —"

Before she could finish Kay took out his memory neuralyzer and zapped her. She blinked her eyes, dazed. Jay knew the signs by now. Laurel was suddenly clueless.

"He said there's a galaxy on Orion's Belt?" Kay asked Jay. "That makes no sense."

"That's what he said," replied Jay.

"Uh, hi," interjected the dazed Laurel. "Whoever you guys are, I'm afraid I'm going to have to see some ID if you're going to be in the morgue, okay?"

"Sure, sweetheart," said Kay.

And with that he pulled out his neuralyzer and zapped her again.

12.
Empty Box

Edgar sat in the back of the exterminator van. He was huddled next to his spaceship, Rosenberg's jewelry box on his lap.

He couldn't get the box open, and it was making him angrier by the minute. The box was bent and battered from his several attempts to claw into it.

Nothing, he vowed silently, would stop him from getting what was inside. His very fate depended on it.

Finally, Edgar wedged a screwdriver under the lid of the box and smacked with his fist. It still didn't open.

Now he was really mad. He screamed with rage and hurled the box against the side of the van. When it landed, he noticed that one of its hinges had cracked open. Edgar laughed. He grabbed the box and ripped the lid off with his fingers.

Inside, there was a mound of precious diamonds and glittering jewels. They were worthless to him. What he was looking for was probably underneath. He reached in and threw the jewelry aside.

But the box was empty.

"No!" he screamed in despair. "No, no, no, *noooo!*"

And with that he ripped the box apart with his bare hands.

13.
Mass Departure

Jay was tired. It was early morning before he and Kay returned to MiB headquarters. Despite the hour, the headquarters was still going full blast. The large main screen was displaying the constellation Orion and agents were huddled around it.

"Doesn't anybody believe in sleep around here?" Jay asked Zed as he approached the screen.

"We're on Centaurian time," explained Zed. "Thirty-seven-hour days. Give it a few months, you'll get used to it. Or you'll have a psychotic episode."

Zed pointed to the constellation on the screen. "This is Orion," he said. "The brightest grouping of stars in the northern sky. Those three stars over there are Orion's Belt."

"That's what the little guy was talking about," said Jay. "'To prevent war, the galaxy's on Orion's Belt...'"

"There *are* no galaxies on Orion's Belt," said Zed. "The Belt is just these three stars. Galaxies are huge, made up of *billions* of stars. You heard wrong."

Jay frowned and tried to remember more clearly what the little man in Rosenberg's head had tried to say. Then he looked around for Kay, who was sitting in front of a video console across the room.

Kay looked tired. His tie was loosened, his shoulders sagged slightly. On the screen before him was the image of a woman who looked to be around Kay's age, whatever that was. Location: Arizona.

"Pretty lady," said Jay.

The woman was in her backyard, setting up a picnic table.

It didn't take long for Jay to figure out why Kay was looking at the woman. He remembered the photos Kay showed him of the first arrival of the aliens. As a young man, Kay had brought flowers to greet the aliens. Now Jay realized those flowers were meant for someone else.

"Were you on your way to a dance or something?" Jay asked Kay. "She never got those flowers, did she?"

Kay didn't answer. Instead, he just stared at the screen.

"She ever get married?" asked Jay.

"No," replied Kay. Then he reached over and turned the monitor off.

"Kay," called Zed. Kay and Jay went over to the main monitor.

"They're leaving," said Kay when he saw the monitor. One by one the tiny lights that represented the landed aliens worldwide were disappearing.

"We've had twelve jumps in the last hour," said Zed. "Redgick was just the beginning."

"What do they know that we don't know?" asked Jay.

"Why do rats desert the ship?" asked Kay. He ordered that the monitor's image be changed to a forty-field view of Manhattan.

"Increase to four thousand," ordered Kay. The image changed again. This time it was a view of the earth in space. Kay stepped in closer to the screen. Something was wrong.

"That's an Arquillian battle cruiser," he said, pointing at an area on the screen.

"And we've got a dead Arquillian prince," added Zed ominously. "Kay, get down to Rosenberg's store and see what you can turn up. And, Kay —"

Having already started off, Kay and Jay stopped and turned around before leaving.

"— take a lot of firepower."

Kay heeded his commander's advice and led Jay downstairs to an equipment locker. He pulled out a huge multibarreled handgun.

"Now you're talking!" said Jay, eager to have one of his own.

"Series four de-atomizer," said Kay as he put the gun into his holster. Then he handed Jay the tiniest gun in the locker. It looked like something that came out of a gumball machine. "Here," said Kay. "We call this the Noisy Cricket."

"You get a series four de-atomizer and I get a Noisy Cricket?" exclaimed Jay. "I'm afraid I'm going to break it." Kay didn't even crack a smile. Instead, he led Jay outside to the car.

In minutes they were speeding uptown.

14.
Encounter with a Bug

Edgar wouldn't let a little thing like one lock stop him, let alone five locks. He pulled back his fist and smashed it through the window of Rosenberg's Jewelry Store. It was night. The street was deserted. Nobody heard a thing.

Edgar reached inside and quickly unlatched each of the five locks that were meant to keep the store safe from burglars. Then he went inside.

The store was a treasure trove of expensive gems, bracelets, watches, necklaces, and rings. Even in the night light their glitter made Edgar blink.

Where to begin?

Edgar reached over the counter and grabbed a handful of jewels, inspecting the bunch as he did so.

Nothing. He threw the jewels away.

Somewhere around here . . .

He went through the store scooping up handfuls

of jewelry, examining them, each time coming up empty. They were worthless.

Edgar became angry. He hadn't expected Rosenberg to be that smart. He began smashing everything in sight, even the framed pictures on the walls. He stopped at one picture. The cat. Nice picture. And there was more than one. The wall was filled with pictures of this cat. Rosenberg was hopelessly sentimental.

From outside came the sound of a truck. Edgar swerved around. Some vehicle was pulling up to his van. It had a long pole and hook sticking out from its top. The words *City Tow* were written across its side. Within minutes his van was being hoisted up by the tow truck.

Edgar went back outside and crossed the street. "That's my van!" he yelled at the tow-truck driver.

"Make sure you tell them that at the impound," the driver shot back.

Edgar curled his lip. He went over to the van and pulled his farm rifle out from under the front seat. Then he pointed it at the tow-truck driver.

The driver smiled, unafraid. "I got worse in the truck," he said, pulling a shotgun off the seat beside him.

That didn't stop Edgar. He stepped toward the driver.

The driver cocked his shotgun. It was the last

thing he did before the tentacle shot out of Edgar's sleeve and grabbed him around the throat.

Edgar lifted the driver out of the truck. The driver gasped for air. Then his fingers weakened and the shotgun slipped from his grasp. Edgar released his slimy grip and let the driver fall to the ground.

Jay barely noticed the commotion across the street. Guys were always arguing with the city tow boys. Never did any good. If they got your vehicle, they got it. Didn't matter if you were right or they were right. Bottom line was the same. It always came out of your pocket.

Besides, the mess was too distracting. Someone had smashed Rosenberg's storefront to bits. And inside it wasn't any better. Funny thing though. The place had been ransacked, but no jewels were taken.

"Who robs a jewelry store and leaves the jewels?" asked Jay.

"Someone who's not looking for jewels," replied Kay. Both of them were stepping through the heaps of discarded jewelry and broken glass.

Jay stopped at a wall. Pictures of a cat. Lots of them. Nearby was a pile of bejeweled cat collars. He picked one up and examined it. "This guy had a serious crush on his cat," he said.

Through the window Jay saw someone walking

toward the store. He wondered if it was a looter. It was only a matter of time before the looters showed up.

The figure got closer. It was a man. A big, lumbering man. And he was armed with a rifle in one hand, a shotgun in the other.

Jay knew the man. That is, he had seen his picture somewhere before. His mind quickly raced through the hundreds of images he knew from the police mug-shot book. Too many. But there was something about this man. Something special. Something familiar, like he had seen the picture recently. Like in someone's house.

Like in Edgar's house.

"Kay!" Jay shouted a warning. "Get down!"

Edgar had reached the store and had both guns aimed right at Jay and Kay. Kay hit the ground. Jay raised his Noisy Cricket, aimed, and fired.

The blast was as loud and powerful as a bazooka. It hurled Jay back a good ten feet, slamming him into the wall of cat pictures with tremendous force.

The shot missed Edgar, but it was enough to scare him off. He turned and fled down the street.

"The Bug in the Edgar suit," Jay said as Kay helped him to his feet. "The ugly redneck from the picture! That was him!"

Jay ran after Edgar. Kay followed.

By the time they reached the street, Edgar was roaring away in the tow truck, the exterminator van dragging behind. Jay ran into the middle of the street, got down on one knee, braced himself, aimed carefully, and fired the Noisy Cricket again. This time the great blast from the tiny gun hit the rigging between the tow truck and the van, separating the two.

The tow truck was just about to turn a corner when Jay leaped onto a parked car and aimed his gun again. But this time another truck backed up in front of him, blocking his view. By now it was too late. Jay had pulled the trigger. The new truck exploded to bits. Jay went flying backward and crashed across the hood of a passing car.

He was on the ground for several minutes before he saw Kay's face leaning over him.

"We don't discharge our weapons in front of civilians," said Kay flatly.

"That's why *you* do not catch Edgar," Jay replied angrily.

"We've got exposure here that needs to be contained," said Kay.

"Can we drop the cover-up double-talk?!" insisted Jay. "There's an alien battle cruiser that's gonna blow up the world if we don't —"

"There's *always* an alien battle cruiser, or a Korlian death ray, or an intergalactic plague about to wipe out life on this planet," explained Kay. "The only thing that lets people get on with their hopeful little lives is that *they don't know about it.*"

By now several onlookers had crowded onto the street and were looking at the demolished truck and storefront. Jay silently conceded Kay's point. He stood up.

"Don't worry," said Kay. He had walked over to the exterminator van. "That Bug's not leaving town."

"How do you know?" asked Jay.

Kay opened the back door of the van and pointed at the craft inside.

"Because we've got his spaceship."

15.
Frank the Pug

"**T**he exodus continues," Kay was told by Zed when he called headquarters from a pay phone. One by one the little lights on the world map at MiB headquarters were going out. One by one, about one every five or ten minutes. The aliens were fleeing Earth. Even some of the aliens that worked at MiB had packed their suitcases and were leaving. "It's like the party's over and the last one to leave gets stuck with the check."

"What about the Arquillians?" asked Kay.

"We've only translated a part of the message so far," replied Zed. "*Deliver the galaxy.*'"

"Great," sighed Kay hopelessly.

"Oh, it gets better," said Zed. "Another contestant has entered the ring."

Kay listened, then hung up. He turned to Jay. "Bad news," he reported. "Got a second hostile battleship in orbit."

"Lemme guess," quipped Jay. "The little green dude's family."

"Baltians, right," replied Kay. He began thumbing through an address book. "We need help. Someone with a thorough understanding of galactic politics. I just hope he hasn't skipped the planet."

Kay drove crosstown and pulled up in front of a corner hardware kiosk. Behind the counter the vendor was wearing a beat-up old sweater, watch cap, and fingerless gloves. He was a nervous man, full of ticks and mannerisms. Jay couldn't believe it.

"Of course that guy's an alien," he said as he and Kay approached the kiosk. "That's gotta be the worst disguise I've ever seen."

Suddenly the vendor's dog, a small white pug with a flat face, scrunched snout, and big round eyes, came into view.

"Closing early, Frank?" Kay kneeled down and asked the pug.

Jay was completely stunned.

"Sorry, Kay," replied the pug. "I can't talk right now. My ride's leaving in —"

Kay grabbed the pug. "Call the pound! We got a stray," he threatened.

"Hey, get your paws off me," said Frank the Pug, squirming.

"Arquillians and Baltians," Kay barked to the dog. "What do you know?"

Frank could see he was fighting a losing battle. "I know they've been fighting since forever over a third galaxy," he told Kay. "There was a peace conference downtown, and the Baltians were gonna turn over the galaxy. But the Bug had other plans."

"His colony's been living off this war for centuries," Kay explained to Jay. Jay was trying not to look embarrassed at standing next to a man who was talking to a dog.

"Ask him about the belt," suggested Jay.

"Beats me," replied the pug. "I heard the galaxy was here."

"Here?" asked Kay.

"Millions of stars and planets?" asked Jay. "I don't get it."

"You humans," said the pug smugly. "When're you gonna learn that size doesn't matter. Just 'cause something's important doesn't mean it's not very, very small."

"How small?" asked Kay.

"*Tiny*," replied the dog. "Like the size of a marble. Or a jewel. Now, if you'll excuse me, I need to be walked before the flight."

Realizing he'd got what he wanted, Kay released Frank. The pug pulled out a tiny little suitcase from behind the kiosk and scurried away.

"The Baltian didn't say *belt*," said Kay, confused.

"The little green dude," said Jay, thinking aloud. "He was trying to say something, I thought it was *belt*, but his English wasn't so good."

"Maybe he meant something else," said Kay.

Jay thought quickly. Like an alien speaking another language. Take a word. Any word in another language. Could sound like one thing but mean another. Take *belt*, for example. Take anything that may look like a belt, for example.

Jay suddenly realized what the Baltian had meant. He told Kay to drive to the city morgue.

16.
Bug on the Loose

Dr. Laurel Weaver was thinking of calling it a day. She was working late, as she usually did. Work kept her mind occupied. It kept her from feeling so lonely. At home, in the overpriced one-bedroom apartment where she lived alone, it was quiet and lonely. She often joked to herself: The morgue was a quiet place, but at least there were bodies around.

She had just closed a file when the cat jumped on her desk. The cat had made itself quite at home since it was brought in with the two old guys earlier. She stroked the creature's fur. It was friendly enough. Laurel guessed it needed some company, too. Well, she'd often thought about getting a pet.

She fumbled with the tag around the cat's neck. It was more like a marble than a tag. It shimmered in the light. A word was written across it: *Orion*.

"Orion," Laurel said to the cat. "That's a pretty name."

She could not take her eyes off the circular object that hung around Orion's collar. It was hypnotic, made of some kind of strange and beautiful metal. Light green in the center, translucent.

"Wow . . ." muttered Laurel, staring deep into the object. She felt as if she were being sucked into another universe. Around her were millions of stars and planets, all shapes, sizes, and colors. She wanted to remain lost in there forever.

Suddenly her concentration was broken by the sound of the outer doorbell.

Orion snarled. Her fur stood on end. The cat leaped off the table and scurried away fearfully.

Laurel wasn't sure, but she thought she heard the security guard outside talking to somebody. Then she heard a muffled scream.

Next, strange, heavy footsteps approached her door.

Kay stepped on the gas pedal. The LTD sped closer to the city morgue. It was agreed. Jay and Kay weren't looking for a belt in the sky. They were looking for something that looked like a belt. And it had to be something connected to the dead Baltian, Rosenberg.

It was the collar around the neck of Rosenberg's cat. Had to be.

"So two galaxies have been fighting for years," said Jay, trying to make sense of it all. "And the only people who've been benefiting are a race of creatures called Bugs. Then the two galaxies decide to make peace and the Bugs send this guy down to make sure the fighting *never* stops."

"By killing emissaries and stealing the galaxy they've been fighting about," added Kay.

"And if we don't get that galaxy back before the Bug leaves the planet, *we're* history."

"We're not even history," said Kay. "Because history implies there's gonna be someone around to remember it."

They reached the city morgue and got out of the car.

"I'll handle this one," Jay told Kay. "You wait outside."

"Why?"

"Because all we have to do is walk in and get a cat, it's not that hard," Jay snapped. "But if *you* go in, you're gonna end up erasing half that woman's med-school classes with that neuralyzer of yours. She doesn't need that."

Kay agreed. He gave Jay two minutes.

"Where is the animal?" the man demanded a second time. The first time was when he had burst into the office seconds earlier. Dr. Weaver had never seen the farmer before, but something told her she was in immediate danger.

"I *told* you," she insisted. "I don't know. It ran under some equipment. Over there!"

"*Get* it!" ordered the farmer.

Then he grabbed the medical examiner and dragged her across the morgue to the area she had been pointing at. Dr. Weaver reached behind some equipment. A second later, Orion came scurrying out, leapfrogged across the room, and jumped on top of some tall file cabinets.

The farmer started toward Orion, then froze.

Someone had just rung the doorbell.

"Hello?" Jay's voice was heard from outside. "Anybody there?"

The farmer looked at Dr. Weaver. He warned her to keep quiet. Then he hid beneath an examining table.

Before long, Jay entered the room.

"Hi," he said to Dr. Weaver.

Dr. Weaver remained rigid. "Hello," she said flatly.

"I'm Sergeant Friday from the twenty-sixth precinct," said Jay, flashing a fake badge. "They brought a cat in here with a corpse the other day. Might have said *Orion* on the name tag?"

"Yes," replied Laurel weakly. "That's right."

"Well, that cat's a witness in a murder case," explained Jay. "I'm going to need to take it with me."

"I don't know where the cat is at the moment."

"You don't?"

"No," said Dr. Weaver. Then she added quietly: "Maybe you could take *me* with you instead."

Jay paused, momentarily taken aback. "*Excuse* me?" he asked.

"I said, maybe you could take me with you instead," repeated Laurel. "I'd really like to go with you. Now."

Jay was stunned. He was pretty good at getting women to like him, but he was never *this* good. "Why is that?" he asked Laurel.

"I have something to show you," replied the medical examiner.

But no sooner had she said that than the examining table in front of her shot up into the air. The man in the farm clothes grabbed Dr. Weaver and aimed his shotgun at her.

Jay's heart jumped. He recognized the man at once.

It was Edgar. The Bug.

17.
Face-off

Without warning, the door burst open. It was Kay. And he was aiming his series four deatomizer at the Bug. *"Freeze it, Bug!"* he shouted.

"Don't shoot! Don't shoot!" Jay shouted at Kay.

"Man, you are thick!" Laurel shouted at Jay, her hands grasping at Edgar's arms.

"How was I supposed to know?" replied Jay, embarrassed.

"What did I have to do? Sing it for you?"

"Everybody shut up!" shouted Edgar.

"Let her go!" Kay ordered Edgar, his gun still aimed at the Bug.

"Listen, monkey boy," said Edgar, poking the barrel of his shotgun toward Laurel. "I may have to take that kind of talk in my end of the universe, but compared to you humans, I'm on the top rung of the evolutionary ladder, *so can it!*"

"You're breakin' my heart," said Kay. He cocked his weapon. "Move six inches to your left and I'll solve all your problems."

Just then something streaked through the air. Orion. A shooting star made of fur and claw. It landed on Edgar, hissing and scratching away. Edgar snapped his arm around and grabbed the cat. Then he saw the glittering object that hung from Orion's collar.

Jay saw it, too. All of a sudden he realized what Frank the Pug had meant by the galaxy being right here. Millions and millions of stars and planets. Tiny. Right here. Hanging from Orion's collar.

The galaxy was *inside* that circular object.

And now Edgar had it. In a split second he had put it into his mouth and swallowed it. Then he jammed his gun even harder into Dr. Weaver's cheek. Jay and Kay backed off.

"That's better," said Edgar. "Now put down your weapons. We're leaving."

Jay put his gun down, but Kay remained frozen, his gun still outstretched before him.

Edgar twisted Dr. Weaver's arms. "Have you ever pulled the wings off a fly?" he asked Kay, threatening to do something just like that to Dr. Weaver. "Would you care to see the fly get even?"

"How far do you expect to get without your ship?" Kay asked the Bug. "If that's what you call that hunk of space crap we've got back at our office."

"Put the weapon down!" demanded Edgar.

"Never gonna happen, insect," said Kay.

Edgar began to back away.

"It's okay, Laurel," said Jay.

"*How* is it okay?" shouted Laurel, helpless.

"I mean it's *going* to be okay," said Jay.

"Don't bet on it, meat sack," said Edgar. And with that the Bug jumped backward and went crashing through the window.

Kay and Jay ran outside, but they were too late. Edgar had pulled a taxi driver out of a cab. Then, forcing Dr. Weaver to drive, he escaped down the street.

Jay started running after the cab, but soon it disappeared from sight.

"Stop wasting time," Kay called out to Jay. "He's not getting off this planet in a cab."

Jay nodded, ran back to Kay, and followed him into their car.

18.
Alien Face-off

Kay and Jay returned to MiB headquarters, their weapons ready. But all was quiet. Edgar was not there. His spaceship remained in its cage, confiscated, untouched.

"Maybe he's not coming here," said Jay.

"He *has* to," said Kay. "There's no other way off the planet."

Just then a loud warning buzz came from the main observation screen. They hurried over. Zed was already there. On the screen everyone could see that both the Arquillian battleship and the Baltian battle cruiser had taken position on either side of Earth.

"We've still got the Arquillian ship parked above us," Zed told Kay and Jay. "And now there's a Baltian ship in oppositional orbit with it!"

"The Arquillians are demanding the return of the Third Galaxy," reasoned Kay aloud.

"That's right," said Zed.

"And the Baltians say they don't have it and want to know what happened to their high prince," finished Kay.

Zed nodded. "That's the gist of it, from what we've been able to interpret," he said. "Tempers are running rather high."

Suddenly a red line shot out from the Arquillian ship, headed straight for the Baltian ship. To reach the enemy vessel, the red line seared through the center of Earth itself.

Alarms went off everywhere.

"That can't be good," said Jay.

"The Arquillian just sent a torpedo through the North Sea," said Zed.

Next, the Baltians sent a beam back at the Arquillian ship. Again the beam pierced through the planet.

"That one went right through the Gobi Desert," said Zed.

"*Why are they shooting at us?*" asked Jay, panic-stricken.

"Andromeda Convention protocol," explained Zed. "They each get one shot, then they hunker down and try to come to terms."

"Just how much hunkering do they do before it's open season?" asked Jay.

"One hour," said Kay.

"Then what?" asked Jay. "They start gunning it

out with us in the line of fire? Why can't they set-
tle this in their own galaxy?"

"The treaty requires the antagonists to meet in
a part of the universe devoid of intelligent life-
forms," said Zed. "That means us."

"Pull up the locations of all land-based interstellar vehicles," Kay told Zed.

"Already did," replied Zed. "Frank the Pug
took the last ship on the planet."

"Atlantic City?" asked Kay.

"Gone," replied Zed.

"That landfill on the Jersey Shore?"

"Gone."

"Uh, gentlemen," interrupted Jay.

"Epcot?"

"Gone."

"Miami Beach?"

"Gone."

"Fellas," Jay persisted.

"Hartford?"

"Gone," replied Zed.

"Hey, *old guys*," said Jay. His attention had
drifted to a mural of the 1964 World's Fair that
was spread over the computer terminals. "Do
those still work?" He was pointing to the two flying saucers on top of the science exhibit building,
the ones used by the first arriving aliens so many
years ago.

Kay and Zed looked up at the mural. Their expressions were all that Jay needed to convince him that the ships probably did work. They were Edgar's only means of escape.

"Whaddya say we bag us some Bug?" Kay asked Jay.

Jay nodded eagerly. Then they raced outside, leaped into the LTD, and roared toward Queens.

19.
Traffic Jam

The Midtown Tunnel, as Jay warned, was jam-packed with cars leaving Manhattan.

"I told you the tunnel would be jammed," he said to Kay as they approached the tunnel.

But Kay wasn't concerned. "The button."

Jay was surprised. He hadn't forgotten Kay's express instruction never to touch the red button that was located between them. But Kay was insistent.

"Push the button, Jay," said Kay. "And you *may* want to throw on a seat belt."

The button popped up from its protective plastic shield. Jay reached for it and pushed hard.

Jay felt a sudden roar of power beneath him. The LTD began to vibrate. Then he felt a swooping dizziness. He looked down and noticed the dashboard seemed to be changing its shape. It stretched and pulled as if it were made of Silly Putty. Next the sides and back of the car extended and turned into a larger, more wiry machine. Then it plunged, top speed, into the traffic jam ahead.

But instead of ramming into the cars in front of it, the LTD let itself be sucked into the tunnel. It swerved up on its side and onto the wall of the tunnel and clung there like an agile spider. Then it raced by the traffic below.

The force of the vehicle pushed Jay back into his seat, then dropped him upside down onto the ceiling. He had wanted to scream, but found that his stomach had somehow gotten in the way of his throat.

"Mind if I smoke?" Kay asked casually, unperturbed by the ride.

"*What?!*"

"In the car, I mean."

"*I don't care!*" replied Jay, hoping the ride would be over soon.

In a matter of seconds the car passed through the tunnel and came out on the other side. It flipped over, banged back down on the road, and sped through the tunnel's tollbooth.

Jay slammed back into his seat.

"Well," sighed Kay. "Back to work."

Kay stepped on the gas. The LTD raced along the highway. Within minutes Jay could see the famous globe of the Earth sculpture that stood overlooking the old World's Fair grounds. Kay brought the LTD to a long, skidding stop.

"He's got Laurel!" Jay said, pointing upward.

Kay looked up. Edgar, with Dr. Weaver under

his arm, was climbing one of the towers of the science exhibit. Before long he had reached the landing platform at the top of the tower.

Edgar pushed Laurel ahead of him on the landing tower. He was making his way to the saucer at the top.

"Come on, let me go," begged Laurel as she felt herself being prodded forward. "You don't want to eat me. I'm a very important person on my planet. Like a queen. A goddess, even. There are those that worship me. I'm not trying to impress you with this, I'm just letting you know. It could start a war."

"Good," replied Edgar, unconcerned. "War means food for my family, all seventy-eight million of them. That's a lot of mouths to feed, *your highness*."

Laurel tightened her lips. "You're a wonderful dad," she muttered sharply. With that, she kicked Edgar squarely in the face. Edgar reeled back, momentarily losing his grip on Laurel.

Now free of his grasp, Laurel jumped off the landing platform. She sailed, free-form, through the air. Then her fall was broken by a nearby tree. She hit it hard, but managed to grab a limb and pull herself to safety in its branches.

Jay's heart stopped. He wanted to run to help her. He also wanted to kill that Bug.

Kay flipped open the trunk of the LTD. He and Jay pulled out an array of dangerous-looking weapons. Then Kay grabbed a long black box, unsnapped its cover, and pulled out what looked like three double-barreled shotguns melded into one.

Jay had never seen anything like it before.

"You know how to work that?" he asked Kay.

Kay pumped the weapon once, with confidence. "No idea whatsoever," he replied smugly. Then he slammed down the trunk and said, "Let's bag us some Bug."

Just then they heard a loud hum. They looked up. Edgar had gone inside the spaceship and started it up. It had already begun to spin, slowly at first, then faster and faster.

Then it began to rise.

20.
The Bug Inside Edgar

Kay raised his weapon and aimed it into the night sky in search of Edgar's stolen spaceship.

"Set it to pulsar level five, subsonic implosion factor," he told Jay.

"What?" asked Jay helplessly.

"Press the little green button, on three," said Kay. Jay raised his weapon and located the green button.

"*One . . .*" Kay began counting. "*Two . . .*"

Edgar's ship came into view.

"*Three!*"

Kay and Edgar fired their guns.

Nothing. Not even the sound of a blast.

"What happened?" asked Jay. "Did we miss?"

Kay smiled. Suddenly they heard a loud sucking sound, as if all the air around them were being sucked into space. Then a tremendous shock wave blasted out of their guns. The force of the shock wave was so great that Kay and Jay were thrown to the ground by its pressure.

The shock wave wrinkled up through the atmosphere, hitting Edgar's ship as it passed by. The ship lost its balance, and now it, too, was sucked back down. It came hurtling earthward, crashing through brush, dirt, and rock as it went.

Kay and Jay rose to their feet. They could barely see through a cloud of dirt and dust. When the dust had cleared, the saucer was there, embedded in the earth, tipped off-kilter in a mountain of debris.

Then came the sound of a latch being turned. A hatch popped up from the hull of the ship. Edgar's head poked through. Then his shoulders, then his arms. He climbed out of the spaceship with a mean scowl on his face.

"You don't get it," he told Kay and Jay. "I've won. It's over."

Kay ignored the Bug and aimed his gun. "You are under arrest for violating number four-one-fifty-three of the Tycho Accord," he told Edgar. "Please hand over any galaxy you might be carrying."

"You fools!" laughed Edgar. "You don't matter! In a few seconds you won't even *be* matter!"

"Move away from the vehicle and put your hands on your head," Jay told Edgar. Then he pumped his gun for emphasis.

"Put my hands on my head?" said Edgar. He lifted his arms over his head. "Like this?"

No sooner were Edgar's arms flexed than two giant insectlike pincers burst through the armpits of his rotting skin. The pincers opened and spread out of each side of Edgar's body, each one the length of a small automobile.

Next, the skin and clothes on Edgar's legs began to crack and shred. They burst apart and fell away. Edgar's human legs were gone, but in their place were two double-thick insect legs. Their skin was hard and shiny, more like a shell. Moist brown muscle oozed at the joints.

Edgar took a deep breath, and his chest exploded. His human skin went flying everywhere, revealing more Bug muscle inside. Finally, his head exploded away and spattered all around. His new head was huge, with two antennae jutting from its top. Now Edgar stood before Kay and Jay in all his alien glory. A giant, hairy, insectlike creature as ugly as any they had ever seen. And around his neck hung the translucent orb that held the Third Galaxy.

Kay and Jay aimed their guns at the Bug. The Bug curled back its hundreds of sharp teeth and spat out a huge gob of slimy brown goo. The goo wrapped itself around both shotguns and the Bug yanked them away. The Bug swallowed both guns whole. Then it raised a pincer and slapped Kay and Jay away as if it were brushing aside a mosquito.

"That did not go at all as I planned," said Jay, after hitting the ground a good fifteen feet away.

Kay and Jay stood up. They saw the Bug running back toward the science tower. It was going to try to escape in the second flying saucer.

"That guy's really starting to bug me," said Kay. Then he started after the Bug. "Whatever happens, Jay, don't let him get on that ship."

"What are you doing?" asked Jay, following.

"Getting my gun back," Kay said flatly.

"What?!"

"Hey, Bug!" Kay shouted out. But the Bug ignored him and kept lumbering toward the tower. Kay continued: "I'm talking to you, Bug! You know how many of your kind I've swatted with a newspaper?"

At that the Bug stopped and turned around. Kay had gotten to it.

"You're just a smear on the sports page to me," he continued taunting. "You slimy, gut-sucking intestinal parasite!"

Without warning the Bug opened its giant jaw, leaned forward, and sucked Kay into its mouth.

21.
Man Versus Bug

"**K**ay —!" shouted Jay, stunned. He watched in horror as the Bug swallowed Kay whole. Then it stood up straight and led out a hideous scream of triumph.

Jay felt his legs go weak. He was powerless against this creature and he knew it. How could it be otherwise? After all, he was only human. In the end, what could he do against creatures from other worlds? Kay had been wrong about him. Maybe he wasn't up to the task of being a member of the Men in Black after all.

Call it years of street smarts. Call it years of police training. Or just call it instinct. At that instant something strange caught Jay's eye. The Bug's stomach was moving. Something inside was making the ugly creature's stomach swell and extend in all different directions. Jay wasn't certain, but when the stomach extended a certain way he thought he could make out Kay's face. When it extended another way, he could see Kay's hands. Yet again he could make out the faint form of the weapons the Bug had swallowed.

Jay quickly became convinced that Kay was alive inside that giant roach's stomach. Just as quickly, he realized that Kay had allowed himself to be swallowed by Edgar. Kay was trying to get his hands back on the guns. Kay was going to blast the Bug from the inside out!

Jay knew what he had to do. He had to give Kay time. A distraction. Of any kind. Keep that Bug from getting to the spaceship. He picked up a chunk of concrete and threw it at the Bug. The rock bounced off the creature's shell as if off rubber.

"Hey!" he shouted to the Bug, running toward it.

The Bug roared with anger and kicked Jay, sending him flying across the grass.

Then the Bug raised one of its clawlike pincers and sliced it downward. Jay rolled out of the way, between the Bug's legs. Jay groped around for something — anything he could use as a weapon. He found it. A sharp metal spike blown there when the Bug's ship had crashed.

Jay grabbed the spike with both hands and aimed at the center of the Bug's gut. It was too late. The Bug saw him and leaned over. It craned its neck between its legs and snapped its jaws at Jay. Jay propelled himself out of the way, narrowly escaping being eaten alive.

The Bug obviously thought it was free of the human pest. It turned around and resumed its march to the science tower.

Jay watched helplessly. Kay must be having trouble getting a hold on the guns. Time was running out.

"What are you, afraid of me?" Jay shouted, taunting the Bug. "Come on! Stand and fight like an anthropoid!" He screamed and made a running leap right onto the Bug's hard-shelled back.

"You want a piece of this, huh?" challenged Jay while trying to drag the Bug down to the ground. "Maybe you're a big Bug in your hive, but this is New York City. You're just another tourist here."

The Bug flicked its tail and sent Jay sailing twenty feet through the air. When he landed, Jay found himself in a Dumpster, sitting on a heap of garbage.

But he wouldn't let a little garbage stop him. He climbed out of the Dumpster and wiped himself off.

"You're messing with the wrong species, Bug," he said.

Suddenly Jay noticed something crawling on his arm. A cockroach. His first instinct was to flick it off. Something made him fight that urge. He looked down at the ground. There was another roach. Then another and another. In fact, there was a whole convention of roaches climbing in and around a small rusted hole in the Dumpster.

Idea.

A desperate idea.

Jay walked back to the corroded Dumpster and began kicking at it. He kicked again and again. Soon the bolts in the rusted joints of the large garbage box loosened. The Dumpster collapsed and crumbled to pieces.

And out poured thousands and thousands of roaches. A whole mob of them. It was like a sea of shiny, crawling critters.

And they were so helpless.

"Hey, Bug!" Jay called out to the giant alien. It had just started to make its climb up the tower ladder toward the spaceship.

"Hey, Bug!" Jay called again. The Bug stopped and turned.

As soon as he was sure the Bug was watching, Jay lifted his foot and stepped on one of the roaches scurrying beneath him.

"If I'm not mistaken, that was a cousin of yours," he told the Bug with a smile. Then he stepped on another roach. *SCRUNCH!* "Whoa! That had to hurt," Jay said tauntingly. "And what d'you know, here's your Uncle Bob!" *CRUNCH!*

The Bug flinched, obviously hating the sound of dying roaches. Jay could see the anger burning in the Bug's eyes.

Jay hoped he was giving Kay the time he needed to blast the Bug to bits. He stepped forward toward the tower, crunching another roach as he went.

The Bug began to climb down the tower. He moved toward Jay. Now Jay could see Kay's outline in the Bug's stomach, still groping to grab hold of the gun.

"Ooh, there's a pretty one!" said Jay as he chased another roach. "That one looks familiar, doesn't it? I think I know who that is! That's your *mama*!" He raised his foot over the tiny bug.

The Bug had reached Jay now. But Jay kept his eyes focused sharply on the Bug's stomach. He was sure he could see the outline of Kay's hand close around the trigger of one of the de-atomizers. Then Jay heard the weapon cock.

"Good-bye, Edgar," he whispered.

And with that the Bug's midsection exploded from the inside out. The Bug burst in half, its rear section going one way, its head another. Its gooey internal organs spewed out all over Jay. And with them came Kay, a smoking de-atomizer in his hand.

Jay helped Kay to his feet. Both men sighed with relief.

Then something bounced off Jay's foot. He looked down. What was left of the sea of cockroaches had scattered. A glistening round orb had pummeled through them, scaring them away. Jay bent down and picked it up.

Kay smiled. He took out his cell phone and dialed. "Zed," he said when headquarters answered. "Get a message to the Arquillians. We have the galaxy."

22.
MiB No More

"Getting eaten?!" exclaimed Jay as he wiped alien bug goo off his shirt. "That was your plan?"

Kay shrugged and closed his cell phone. "It worked."

"Yeah," said Jay. "After I got my guts beaten out of me!"

"And I almost got digested," said Kay. "It goes with the job."

"You could have told me what you were doing!"

"There wasn't time, sport!"

Just then they heard a loud hiss behind them. They turned. It was the Bug! Its top half was still alive. Its huge jaws were open and coming toward them.

Then *boom!* The Bug's top half exploded into a million bits.

Jay and Kay were stunned. Someone else had shot the Bug. They turned around and saw Dr.

Weaver standing behind them, a smoking de-atomizer in her hand.

"Interesting job you guys have," she said.

Jay realized that Dr. Weaver had seen every-thing from her perch in the tree. That was lucky for them, but not so lucky for her. He knew that Kay would have to wipe her memory clean.

Kay had Jay quickly usher Dr. Weaver into the backseat of their car. Then he drove to headquarters.

Dr. Weaver remained in the car for several minutes after they reached the MiB building. Jay had gotten out and pulled Kay out of earshot. Kay had already taken out his memory neuralyzer.

"Look," he began. "I know we have all these rules, but she did bust the Bug for us and besides, you do that flashy thing to her one more time and she might not remember her own zip code."

Kay remained silent. He set his neuralyzer for maximum.

"Who's she gonna tell anyway?" Jay asked pleadingly. "She only hangs out with dead people."

Kay held up the neuralyzer. "Not her," he said. "Me."

Jay paused. Kay's meaning suddenly became clear. He was going to use the neuralyzer on himself. He looked up at the evening sky.

"They're beautiful, aren't they?" he asked Jay.

"You all right, man?" asked Jay.

"The stars," Kay continued. "I never just look anymore."

By now Dr. Weaver had gotten out of the car. "Hey, guys," she said, approaching the two Men in Black. "We're nowhere near my apartment."

But Jay was still looking at Kay. "I can't do this job alone," he said.

"Maybe you won't have to," replied Kay, walking over to Dr. Weaver. He put his finger on top of Laurel's name tag, covering all the letters in her name except the "L."

"Elle . . ." he said. "That'll work."

Next, Kay pointed to the notches on the neuralyzer. "Hours. Days. Years," he instructed Jay. "Always set it forward." Then he took out his sunglasses and told Dr. Weaver to put them on. Jay hesitated before putting on his own.

"I've just been down the gullet of an interstellar cockroach," said Kay. "You think that's a memory I want to keep?" He handed Jay the neuralyzer. "See you around, sport."

Jay knew what he had to do. He held up the neuralyzer and fired. There was the usual brilliant white flash. When it was over, Jay could tell by Kay's blank expression that his memory of the last thirty years was gone. He was no longer an MiB.

23.
Elle

Jay stood at the newspaper kiosk, open tabloid in his hand, and quickly perused the headlines. A smile immediately came over his face as he found the one he was looking for:

Man Awakens from 30-year Coma — Returns to Girl He Left Behind.

And right beneath the headline was a photo. A man and a woman, arm in arm, somewhere in Arizona.

Kay, Jay thought to himself happily. *All right.*

Jay folded the paper and returned to the curb where the black LTD was double-parked. His new partner, the woman he once knew as Laurel Weaver, was waiting for him there, leaning against the hood.

She was dressed in black. And now she was called Elle.

"Zed called," said Elle as they got back into the car. "The High Consulate of Regent-nine emissary wants floor seats to the Knicks-Bulls game."

"I'll talk to Dennis Rodman," quipped Jay as he turned the ignition key. "It's his planet."

Elle took the tabloid from Jay and looked it over. From the headlines she could tell it was going to be a busy day.

"Let's roll," she said.

Jay dropped the car into gear and roared away down the streets of Manhattan.

Epilogue:
Out of This World

The LTD is just one of many cars on a jam-packed Manhattan street.

From up above, Manhattan is just part of a much larger city surrounded by suburb after suburb.

From the stratosphere, the east coast of the United States is just part of a much larger land mass.

From the eosphere, North America is just a small portion of the planet Earth.

From space, Earth is just a tiny ball in our solar system.

From the middle of the Milky Way, our solar system is just a few blips of light in a vast star field.

From *outside* our galaxy, the Milky Way is just a creamy spiral of stars amid many other spirals of stars.

From the outer reaches of the universe, everything that exists seems to be contained in one tiny ball, one marble, resting on a patch of red dirt.

An inhuman hand, an alien hand, reaches down and flicks the marble, sending it skittering and bouncing across the dirt, where it clicks into a dozen other big blue balls just like it.